PR

'Murugan's fictional villages are places that are patriarchal, where caste boundaries are protected with violence and social exclusion ... [*Pyre* is] so tense it leaves you gasping for air'—Ellen Barry, *New York Times*

'*Pyre* glows with as much power as [*One Part Woman*] did, and adds immeasurable value to contemporary Indian literature ... "Meditative, joyous, humbling"—three words [that] describe perfectly the sensations with which you put down Perumal Murugan's *Pyre*, a book marked with the same quality of luminous integrity and beauty seen in *One Part Woman* ... Aniruddhan translates with a fine ear that preserves beautifully the music of the original ... [Murugan] succeeds in universalising Kongu Nadu to such a degree that place and person fall away and all that remains is a hard and glittering gem of a story'—Vaishna Roy, *The Hindu*

'[A] sensitive, richly textured translation by Aniruddhan Vasudevan ... Murugan writes with a gentle, sensual tenderness that is unforgettable [and also] with cinematic power, and the final images of *Pyre* will sear your heart, though he makes sure that the reader writes the ending with him ... *One Part Woman* was met with intolerance of such a degree that it forced him into silence. *Pyre*, written before the storm of bigotry swept through the author's life, is even more accomplished, bitterly haunting, a love story, and an indictment of those who hate with such staunch righteousness'—Nilanjana Roy, *Business Standard*

'The prose is deceptively simple and sparse. And yet it has the effect of hitting you hard like the blazing sun ... [Murugan] knows how to handle masterful imagery and human emotions. Especially when he delves into the emotional space of his women characters, be it a coarse, unloving mother-in-law or the soft, sparrow-like, bewildered new bride . . . A sensitive translation done with great care. There is not a single word that jars . . . [*Pyre*] will haunt the reader for a long time'—Vaasanthi, *Indian Express*

'The real fire in *Pyre* [lies] in Murugan's words . . . Aniruddhan Vasudevan [translates] the story of *Pyre* beautifully . . . With *Pyre*, Murugan places a love story at the centre of human confusion and regional literature at the centre of Indian mainstream writing'—*Financial Express*

'A poignant love story . . . Murugan vividly describes the dusty, beautiful landscape and through his characters gives us a peek into the daily struggles and joys of a different kind of life'—*Femina*

PRAISE FOR *ONE PART WOMAN*

'A superb book in which tenderness, love and desire kindle each other into a conflagration of sexual rapture'—Bapsi Sidhwa

'Perumal Murugan opens up the layers of desire, longing, loss and fulfilment in a relationship with extraordinary sensitivity and surgical precision'—Ambai

'A fable about sexual passion and social norms, pleasure and the conventions of family and motherhood . . . A lovely rendering of the Tamil'—*Biblio*

'Perumal Murugan turns an intimate and crystalline gaze on a married couple in interior Tamil Nadu. It is a gaze that lays bare the intricacies of their story, culminating in a heart-wrenching denouement that allows no room for apathy . . . *One Part Woman* is a powerful and insightful rendering of an entire milieu which is certainly still in existence. [Murugan] handles myriad complexities with an enviable sophistication, creating an evocative, even haunting, work . . . Murugan's writing is taut and suspenseful . . . Aniruddhan Vasudevan's translation deserves mention—the language is crisp, retaining local flavour without jarring, and often lyrical'—*The Hindu Business Line*

'An evocative novel about a childless couple reminds us of the excellence of writing in Indian languages . . . This is a novel of many layers; of richly textured relationships; of raw and resonant dialogues and characters . . . Perumal Murugan's voice is distinct; it is the voice of writing in the Indian languages rich in characters, dialogues and locales that are unerringly drawn and intensely evocative. As the novel moves towards its inevitable climax, tragic yet redemptive, the reader shares in the anguish of the characters caught in a fate beyond their control. It is because a superb writer has drawn us adroitly into the lives of those far removed from our acquaintance'—*Indian Express*

'Murugan imbues the simple story of a young couple, deeply in love and anxious to have a child, with the complexities of convention, obligation and, ultimately, conviction . . . An engaging story'—*TimeOut*

'*One Part Woman* has the distant romanticism of a gentler, slower, prettier world, but it is infused with a sense of immediacy . . . Murugan intricately examines the effect the pressure to have a child has on [the couple's] relationship . . . *One Part Woman* is beautifully rooted in its setting. Murugan delights in description and Aniruddhan translates it ably'—*Open*

PRAISE FOR PERUMAL MURUGAN

'Versatile, sensitive to history and conscious of his responsibilities as a writer, Murugan is . . . the most accomplished of his generation of Tamil writers'—*Caravan*

'[A] great literary chronicler . . . Murugan is at the height of his creative powers'—*The Hindu*

'Murugan's insights about relationships spread throughout his work like flashes of lightning'—*Kalachuvadu*

'The Tamil Irvine Welsh'—*Guardian*

PENGUIN BOOKS
CURRENT SHOW

Perumal Murugan is the star of contemporary Tamil literature, having garnered both critical acclaim and commercial success for his work. An award-winning writer, poet and scholar, he has written several novels, short-story collections, poetry anthologies and works of non-fiction. Some of his novels have been translated into English to immense acclaim, including *Seasons of the Palm*, which was shortlisted for the Kiriyama Prize in 2005, and *One Part Woman*, his best-known work, which was shortlisted for the Crossword Award and won the prestigious ILF Samanvay Bhasha Samman in 2015. Murugan has also received awards from the Tamil Nadu government as well as from Katha Books.

V. Geetha is a feminist historian and publisher who writes in English and Tamil on contemporary Tamil society, particularly on caste, gender, education and labour. She translates poetry and fiction from and into both languages. Geetha is with Tara Books, Chennai.

Current Show

PERUMAL MURUGAN

Translated by V. GEETHA

PENGUIN BOOKS

PENGUIN BOOKS

USA | Canada | UK | Ireland | Australia
New Zealand | India | South Africa | China

Penguin Books is part of the Penguin Random House group of companies whose addresses can be found at global.penguinrandomhouse.com

Published by Penguin Random House India Pvt. Ltd
7th Floor, Infinity Tower C, DLF Cyber City,
Gurgaon 122 002, Haryana, India

First published in Tamil as *Nizhal Muttram* by Kalachuvadu Publication Pvt. Ltd, Nagercoil 1993
First published in English by Tara Books Pvt. Ltd, Chennai 2004
Published in Penguin Books by Penguin Random House India 2017

Copyright © Perumal Murugan 2017
English translation copyright © Tara Books Pvt. Ltd 2017

All rights reserved

10 9 8 7 6 5 4 3 2 1

This is a work of fiction. Names, characters, places and incidents are either the product of the author's imagination or are used fictitiously and any resemblance to any actual person, living or dead, events or locales is entirely coincidental.

ISBN 9780143428350

Typeset in Adobe Caslon Pro by Manipal Digital Systems, Manipal
Printed at Thomson Press India Ltd, New Delhi

This book is sold subject to the condition that it shall not, by way of trade or otherwise, be lent, resold, hired out, or otherwise circulated without the publisher's prior consent in any form of binding or cover other than that in which it is published and without a similar condition including this condition being imposed on the subsequent purchaser.

www.penguin.co.in

*To my friends in the cinema hall
who taught me all about life*

Current Show

The young man slumps against a lamp post.

A buzzing aura of insects around his face.

Some spiral down to their deaths, scorched by the heat of the lamp. Rasping, they fall on his chest, arms and legs. He doesn't throw them off. Or make an attempt to move away. He lies, staring at the makeshift shop in front of him.

The shop: a broken cot with a board nailed to it. Small, fat mangoes heaped in a corner. Bottles of sticky boiled sweets sitting uncertainly on the edge. From a distance, they look filled with colour. Like a palm fan, the old cot-shop woman's thin hand, laden with bangles, flaps this way and that, trying to keep the flies away.

Peanuts heaped in a cone. He stares intently at them. A still mess of tiny worms, glistening in the lamplight. He feels a mad desire. Brush that thin waving hand out of the way. Grab the peanuts and run. But to do this, he must get up. He knows he cannot. His legs have gone to sleep. Heavy, wooden.

He looks around him. Dead insects on both sides of his body. What if his body goes stiff forever? He tries to swallow the thick gob of saliva pushing at the walls of his cheeks. It is an effort. In the end, the saliva stays stuck to the roof his mouth. He tightens his lips into a stitch.

A massive back cuts his line of vision and hides the cot-shop. He feels relieved, even thankful. He closes his eyes.

His stomach, worn thin like a cotton rag, pulls into a spasm. His limbs feel like straw. He must find something to eat. How long can this go on? But then, get up—and do what? Maybe he should stretch out and go to sleep.

A hoarse, loud voice startles the evening, shattering its twilight calm. A song. From the film showing in the theatre outside which he lies. The hairs on his forearms rise. His body jerks into tremors. It's a while before it dies down, accepting the blare that hits it.

The theatre lights come on. He looks at the shops inside the theatre compound, to see if there is someone he knows.

Not a fucking baby fly.

~

The song ends.

Quiet for some time, but for a slight whirr. A few moments of static-flecked silence.

Then, BOOM!

The next song. A gravelly voice and a slap of harsh sound.

Over the music from the theatre, another tone slithers into his ears. The old cot-shop woman's wail.

—Take those hands back! Think you can just come and grab what you want? Know what a kilo of peanuts costs? Digging your hands in as if you picked them yourselves! Ask for money and you make faces . . .

His hands itch to strangle her. Choke that voice in her throat. Demon with long, sharp teeth, sitting on her cot and guarding a heap of nuts. She whines on, not stopping to breathe. Stitch that mouth up. Take a huge sack-stitching needle and do it. That fucking song. And her voice that cracks his ears.

No one near the shops yet. No one he knows, at any rate. Maybe his hunger-blurred eyes are playing tricks. Maybe there are people he knows and he can't recognize them.

People are bunching together. A couple. Slowly, more. Soon heads bob outside the queue doors. They grow by the minute, the heads. After a while he can't see the doors.

The crowd is large, spilling on to the road. People at the cot-shop. It is lit by the street lamp which towers over the theatre walls. The old woman has brought her own light. A little oil lamp, whose yellow flicker adds a glow to her wares. She keeps a sharp eye on them.

There are four queue doors opening into the theatre compound, to the ticket counters. The crowd pushes at three of them. The fourth door stands forlorn. Nobody outside. It is never opened. It is brighter and more cheerful than the other doors.

He hears the sound of coins rattling, of shuffling rupee notes. Should he get up and join the crowd? His right hand strays to his shirt pocket. No pocket. Not even the memory of one on the rag he wears. His hand falls back, disappointed.

Clumps of lungi-clad legs pass by. All kinds of lengths and colours. A few pants, some children in shorts. The crowd warms his heart. He feels safe. In any case, who or what can harm him? No one cares for him. He is sure of that.

~

He looks up and sees the film poster lit up by the street lamp.

The hero brandishes a sword. He is about to swing it. His battle skirt billows over his thighs. His mouth is honest. The kind that will address you straight, man to man.

He strains his eyes towards the theatre again. No familiar faces yet. If he could find a rupee, he would stand in the queue like everyone else. He could ask each of them to lend him five paise. That would do.

He wipes the spit away. It comes off on his fingers, black and thick with dirt. He kneads it into pellets and drops them on the ground. Revolted, he lets his eyes run over his chest. His skin is flecked with dirt. Like black moss. No buttons on his ripped shirt. How can he go into the theatre looking like this?

The crowd is bigger now. Why can't one of them look in his direction? Throw a pitying glance and a few coins in its wake? Horrible. Yet the thought haunts him.

Money is money, however you get hold of it. Same value everywhere, for everyone. Will the old cot-shop thing humped over her measly wares part with her peanuts for nothing?

He has to find the strength to reach the crowd. He must. Must put his hands out and beg. No other way.

The theatre bell rings. The moments pass, one by one. With them, the line of heads. The queue doors swallow them into the passages, slowly. Bit by bit. Until there is almost no one left outside. He feels panic. They have left him, cast him to the empty air.

He can see the cot-shop clearly now. The peanut heap has shrunk. The old hag grabs handfuls from a basket next to her and builds the pile up to a new peak. The mangoes—only two left. The oil lamp is snuffed out. Now. Crawl up to the shop, grab the peanuts and run. What if she screams for help? She can't follow him. That's for sure.

But—can he run?

He is filled with self-loathing. Must he lie here forever? Like a pig, with his legs apart?

~

1. They work fast in the darkness
2. The quiet walls echo his call
3. Can't bear being called a beggary dog
4. The well is large and probably very deep
5. His nose has been eaten away to a hollow
6. Sathi kicks at the gate
7. He whirls around, his hands held high
8. A lizard puts out a sly tongue
9. The dice show nothing
10. His voice booms and echoes off the theatre walls
11. He feels sapped and flops back into his seat
12. Laughter echoes around the huge empty room
13. A termite escaping a sudden patch of light
14. Wet sand sits well in ploughed-up areas
15. A dead, dry voice

~

1

They work fast in the darkness

The Hulk lies at the foot of the stairway, his face pressed to the ground. His legs move, keeping time to an unheard beat.

Natesan scribbles numbers on the inside of a cigarette pack, tallying his soda earnings for the day. He stands by the stairway.

Sathivel stands next to Natesan, his back against a wall.

Mani slumps, his legs spread in exhaustion. Now and then, he puffs at a bidi.

Ganesan waits outside the betel-nut shop. He has to hand in his accounts for the day.

The Hulk suddenly lifts his head up.

—Dai, Sathi, looks like you sold a whole lot today!

A faint smile spreads across Sathivel's face. He's in no mood to rise to The Hulk's bait though. Especially since the bastard clearly wants him to say something. But the Hulk insists.

—So, what'd you sell?

—Maybe two dozen. You?

—Oh, less. Less than you. You got a good party in the sofa seats, eh? The buying kind. Shit film's full of sofa-seat types. All come to see what? That Sivaji Ganesan, with his big belly?

—I just managed some cake and coconut bread. Couldn't get rid of the sweets. Not many for the floor and bench seats today.

Mani speaks up. Sathi feels relieved. He's glad Mani has piped up. He doesn't feel like talking to The Hulk.

Sathi's face is always clouded, like his heart hugs a deep sorrow. But he looks better than he did before. He used to go around in ragged shorts and a buttonless shirt. Now he wears a lungi and a T-shirt with faded writing on it. His hair is still the same though. He tries to comb it down, but somehow it springs back up into a dry, messy tangle.

—Our hero's film next week. The Hulk boasts. —Watch me sell . . .

—Keep hoping. It is Mani again. —I'm telling you, that bastard manager's going to bring in some other fucker's film. It's love king Gemini Ganesan or old fart Muthuraman next.

—Dai, Hulk, want to play cards?

Everyone turns to look. It is Ganesan, walking up with a set of playing cards in his hand. He shuffles them several times, setting up a flutter they can't ignore. He stops near Sathi, holds the cards up in front of his face and spreads them out.

Sathi stares at the cards for a moment—then suddenly snatches them from Ganesan. Startled, Ganesan lunges forward and with his thick hands, yanks at Sathi's fingers to get at the cards. Sathi is too quick for him. He runs up and down the staircase and around it. Ganesan runs after him.

The Hulk joins in the chase, trying to snatch the cards from Sathi. Sathi's fist curls tightly around the cards. The Hulk's meaty hand bores into the curled ball of Sathi's fingers, like a pig's snout raking desperately at the earth. He tears Sathi's fist open. His nails peel away the skin around the thumb. Crushed and smeared with sweat, the cards come away in his hands.

—Dai, give them to me, they're mine!

Ganesan pounces on The Hulk.

The Hulk grinds his teeth loudly, waves the cards in the air, tears them into bits and scatters them all around him. He jumps up and down, hooting.

—Motherfucker!

Ganesan sees that the cards are finished.

Sathi sits back against the wall. He is short of breath. He looks at The Hulk, jumping up and down. Huge and menacing. He could bring the theatre down.

—Come on, get some cigarette packs. We'll make our own cards.

The Hulk is genial. The floor of the betel-nut shop is littered with packs. They lie scattered in small white heaps. The boys walk to the shop and start gathering them. They rip the packs open and lay them out, clean insides facing up. Soon they have a stack of white cards.

Sathi goes to the soda shop and returns with a pen. He numbers the smaller cards and starts framing the king, queen and jack. He holds up his king and laughs.

—Aiy, look at this man! Dimpled cheek, chubby face. If he didn't have a moustache, he'd look like The Hulk!

—You mother . . . ! How many times have I told you not to call me The Hulk! You do that once more and I'll tear the flesh from your bones!

The Hulk shakes a massive fist in Sathi's face.

Sathi looks at him in disgust. He'd like to roll him into a ball and fling him outside the theatre gates . . . but his face darkens. He drops the cards and sits quiet.

—Oh, ho! Sweetie-pie's angry!

The Hulk chucks Sathivel under his chin. Sathi pushes his hand away.

—Asshole. Get lost.

The Hulk shuffles away and the others follow him. Sathi stares blankly into the distance.

—That's the problem with you. Get pissed off for nothing. Come on, let's play. You're the one who started drawing the cards!

It is Natesan. He comes up behind Sathi and wraps his arms around him. He lifts him slowly off the ground until Sathi is on his feet. Then he puts his arm around him and, together, they walk past the stairway to the front office. The others are already there, huddled in a corner.

Sounds float out from inside. A song. A long, sad note holds the air. The voice is lost and faraway.

The tea-shop man comes along panting, his egg-roll stomach bobbing up and down. He slips into the theatre. Bare-chested, sweaty, a human hippopotamus.

> *'O fish that dance in the waters of the Vaigai River*
> *O deer that jump nimbly in the rich aromatic forest.'*

Ganesan looks up from his game.

—Aiy, the song! I want to hear it too. You start, I'll be back soon.

—Fucking stupid song. They rush in every time it comes on. To see Fat-face opening and shutting his mouth like a frog . . .

Sathi mutters, dealing out the cards. He takes out a coin and spins it on the floor.

—Start with a 10-paise bet.

—Oy, oy, this game is Natesan's!

Mani croaks, putting out his 10 paise. Cards are flung down and picked up. They giggle and splutter.

—Bastard! That's not fair!

—Go on, get on with it!

They are lost in their game and don't notice Ganesan when he comes out. He stands watching them. From the corner of his eye, he spots the theatre manager.

—Dai, the manager!

He yells and hurtles away around the corner.

The manager comes running, determined to catch them. By the time he reaches the card corner, they have disappeared.

Except for The Hulk. The manager grabs The Hulk by his hair, yanks his head back and slaps him hard on both cheeks, over and over.

—Leftovers-eating dog! Bloody motherfucker! When I ask you to help me let people in at the gate, you run away. And now? Need my theatre to play cards? Where's the rest of your gang?

The Hulk is in pain. It hurts when the manager yanks at his dry, stringy hair. He wriggles to free himself from his sweaty grip.

—Sir, no! No, sir, I was only watching . . .

—I'll speak to your boss about this! Get lost! Where are those other bastards? You'd better bring them to me!

The manager lets go of The Hulk.

He staggers, steadies himself and moves on. He finds an open door and slips into the theatre. The others must be here. Probably hiding in the audience. He looks around and comes out through the exit door on the ladies' side. He sees Natesan and Sathi tiptoeing out of the main gate. He runs after them.

Natesan and Sathivel have become thick, ever since Natesan brought Sathivel in to work with him at the soda shop. Even if they have to piss, they do it together.

When he first came to the theatre, Sathi was quiet and timid. Mani tried to talk the soda-shop owner out of employing him.

—Master, I've seen him before. At Meenal Theatre. He worked there; he's not new or anything . . .

Sathi glared at Mani. His eyes burnt like coals and Mani slapped him hard on the cheek. The soda man tried to get it out of him but Sathi refused to say anything. After a long time he said that he was from Pasavur. When he was asked his name, he muttered, as if saying it to himself.

Somehow Sathi liked Natesan and stuck to him. Maybe because Natesan had found him hungry and weak and had bought him tea and biscuits. When the two got together, they looked at the rest of the world with contempt, as if it wasn't worthy of their attention.

The Hulk is near them.

—We're off to eat, says Sathi. —Manager whacked you?

His mouth curls into a smirk. He makes a face at The Hulk. The Hulk tries to hit him, but Sathivel is quick-footed. He runs ahead, then turns, cuts back and starts to run in circles around Natesan. The Hulk warns him with a finger and yells.

—Know how long I've worked at this theatre? What do you know? You just got here. If you try your fucking games with me . . .

Natesan, who has stayed quiet, cuts him short.

—Ho, ho, ho, don't I know? You steal something, run, then you're back in a day, begging that soda man for a job. I've seen things too . . . fucker.

Sathi stops running. The Hulk is quiet too. He and Natesan catch up with Sathi and they walk silently towards the nearest market town.

The town sits on an incline on the road from Karatur to Sadaiyur.

A little into the road and inside a thick network of dusty alleys stands Sri Vimala Theatre. Its name board is smudged and the letters have long faded into the dust of the incline. The theatre's dull orange walls and bizarre zigzag roof make the building look slightly menacing, like a monstrous anthill. Behind the theatre runs the ring road that links Karatur to Sadaiyur through the town of Aathur.

A mud road leads Sathi, Natesan and The Hulk into the alleyways. Here are arrack shops, little eateries and shacks that sell all sorts of things. Most days, they come here to eat between the evening and the night shows.

The market alley is dark; it has swallowed up the night. It comes alive only on Tuesdays, the local market day. From Monday night, the place hums with life and a festive air. Other times, it is deserted. Then, only dogs, pigs and those whose business needs the cover of dark wander the streets.

The three young men walk through the alleys choked with pigs. Their feet kick angrily at the dried shit—pig and human—scattered all over the place.

The smell of hot prottas from Kaaraan's shop draws them. They usually eat at Kaaraan's. Sathi feels his stomach. Pinched, after an early morning meal eaten before the matinee show. Past the market gate, a splash of light leaps out at them. An ear-splitting tune attacks their ears. They reach Kaaraan's shop.

—What's up? Why so late?

Bathed and glittering in his own sweat, a man stands kneading the protta dough. He greets Natesan amiably. Sathi and The Hulk walk in with half-smiles. They sit and wait for Natesan.

Natesan stands at the entrance. The dough-kneading man asks him something. They whisper together for a long time.

When Natesan finally comes in, the prottas are ready. The man who serves them tears the thick prottas into pieces and drops them on their plates.

Natesan sits next to Sathi and murmurs into his ear.

—The man wants ganja. Can't supply the whole damn world, can we? Siva's gift, he calls it. Ha ha. Okay, but even God's gifts don't last forever and you've got to pay. Hard enough to get hold of it. Easier to drink water through my fucking skull than find the stuff. Tablets, they're different. But I stopped that long ago.

—You used to take tablets?

—Another story. Tell you some other time.

Natesan begins to eat and stops talking. Flies hang in the air, sit on almost everything, marking their presence even at that hour of the night. The Hulk rushes through his protta pieces, spreading his slug-like bulk on the dirty, oily bench.

—Two more!

He yells in the direction of the kitchen and turns to Natesan.

—Dai, give me two rupees, da. It's back with you first thing in the morning—promise! I'll ask my master for some cash.

His big face creases into folds, as he tries to look humble. His eyes plead, small and lost in the thick of his flesh. Natesan feels sorry for him, but shakes his head.

—How about the two rupees you already owe me? No chance. I've got to buy some clothes for myself.

—Dai, I'm telling you, I'll ask the master for money and repay you, da. Please, da!

The place is a furnace. The shop's cement roof radiates heat and its inner walls breathe out a sickly dampness. Beads of sweat bunch on Sathi's upper lip and strain against the new fuzz that has grown on it. He rubs his mouth with the back of his hand and gets up, holding the torn quarter of his lungi so that no one can see the hole. He goes out to wash his hands. Natesan follows him.

—We'll go to the market on Tuesday. I want to buy clothes too.

—That's what you'll say now, Sathi. When the day comes, we won't even have money for God's gift.

They pay, walk out and light bidis. They start to walk slowly towards the market gate. Natesan suddenly remembers and asks Sathi to go and buy two cigarettes.

—They've got a game going near Meenal. Want to go? The Hulk turns to Natesan.

—Look at your face! No money for fucking food and you want to gamble. And you eat so much. What kind of a stomach is that? A bloody cauldron?

—You can't eat because you're always high. I can, because I'm not.

—What's that? I can't eat because I smoke ganja? Say that again, if you've got the balls!

—Not like that! No, no, not like that. I didn't mean it, da.

Sathi returns from the cigarette shop and they walk through the dark market. They stop at an empty stall. Natesan finds a wall and leans against it. The Hulk squats at his feet. Sathi sits close to Natesan.

Sathi taps the tobacco out of a cigarette. He hands the empty paper to Natesan. Natesan has the dust out already, a pinch in the middle of his palm.

Slowly and carefully, he mixes it with tobacco and tilts it into the cigarette paper. Then he twists both ends of the cigarette to a tight point. Sathi opens up the second cigarette. They work fast in the darkness.

The Hulk looks at the joint. He craves it. He mutters, demands. Natesan ignores him. He has finished packing his first one. He pulls at the twisted ends to test if they hold and hands it over to Sathi. He starts on the second.

Something scurries past Natesan and runs over Sathi's feet. He screams, leaps up and sits down again. He wants to catch it—that fucking rat, bat, whatever—and stuff it into The Hulk's shirt. He smiles, imagining The Hulk jumping up and down.

Natesan finishes the second cigarette. Sathi hands the first over to him. Natesan strikes a match. The sound rasps through the dark of the night. The fire sparks and settles into a dull glow at the end of a cigarette. Natesan sits himself back comfortably against the wall and inhales deeply. He draws the smoke in with ease and hands the cigarette back to Sathi.

—Here, don't mess the paper with your spit.

Sathi rests his head on Natesan's thigh and stretches his legs out. He takes two deep draws and returns the cigarette to Natesan. His head spins to a pleasant beat and he laughs. His hand finds a stone and he flicks it at the wall. As the stone falls, Sathi claps and laughs again.

—What are you laughing about?

Natesan pats Sathi on his cheek fondly. Sathi lifts his right hand and presses Natesan's palm to his face. The rough palm provides a safe warmth that spreads slowly to his chest.

Sathi feels his heart go light, as if everything in it has dissolved into a heap of ash. He wants that palm to hold his cheek forever. If it goes away . . . he is afraid to think.

The Hulk continues to cringe and wheedle. He pulls at Natesan's hand and begs.

—Dai, dai, please, da . . .

—Rub my legs then.

Natesan laughs. It is an odd, whirring sound, like a flour-grinding machine. The Hulk is quiet for a few seconds. Then, suddenly, he springs up. His hands work their way down Natesan's legs as he massages them.

—Dai, please. Just one puff, da . . .

—What about my feet?

The Hulk sits on his haunches and runs his hands over Natesan's tight, rough feet.

—Dai, Sathi, tell him to give me just one puff. Da, please!

In the dark, his tone is even more craven, like a shrill night flea that pleads for its life to be spared.

Sathi sits up, leaning on Natesan's shoulder.

—All right, I'll tell him to give you one puff. One condition—you'll do whatever I say.

—Okay, tell me. I'll do it.

—Suck my cock. And his. You'll get it then.

Sathi laughs, arrogant and happy. The Hulk's eyes grow mad.

—Dai!

He grabs Sathi by the front of his T-shirt, lifting him off the ground. The shirt rips as Sathi rolls in the dust.

—Ma!

Sathi moans in pain.

—Son of a whore! Stupid cock!

Natesan grabs The Hulk by his hair and punches him on his face, his back, anywhere he can. The Hulk lifts him up like a kitten and throws him down. They clinch, rolling on their backs in the dust.

Dirty and squashed out of shape, the unlit second joint lies in a corner.

2

The quiet walls echo his call

Like giant snakes, the queue passages twist and wind their way. It is always dark inside them. Sometimes, specks of light get past the queue doors and flee into the theatre. When a show is on, they light the inside faintly. This particular queue passage is never opened to the public though. When it was first built, it was open for a few days—for those who wanted sofa tickets. Even now, a faded board says 'Sofa Ticket: Rs 2.00'. But no tickets are issued. There are not enough people for the sofa tickets and the passage has been closed for years now. No one knows who asked for it to be built and who shut it down. It has become the 'boys' room'.

It is after dawn.

A sharp, black knife of darkness greets the soda man when he comes into the room. His eyes hurt. He rubs them and waits until they get used to the black and then steps inside.

His feet brush against warm flesh. He bends down to see who it is.

A body lies on a film poster. One of the boys. Whoever it is has shrunk into himself, a small tight ball, wrapped in a lungi. A sack of something. Sathi?

The soda man tries to peel the lungi off the sleeping body to catch a glimpse of the face.

Something slithers down his hand. Something creepy. He pulls his hand back and shakes it. He uses his other hand to rub away the feeling. A louse? He bends down again and twitches the lungi from the sleeping face. The Hulk.

He straightens up, disappointed. The Hulk's face twists into a complaint and his hands instinctively pull the lungi back over his face.

The soda man wonders if he should go across, past the sleeping Hulk, to the other side. Should he call out?

—Sathi! Dai, Sathi!

His voice is soft but clear. No one stirs. The quiet walls echo his call. Maybe Sathi isn't even here. Who knows, he could be sleeping inside the theatre. He rubs his eyes and looks around him again. He sees two, no, three tangled bodies—one head on another's thigh, another leg on a third stomach. Is one of them Sathi?

The soda man leans on the wall and jumps over The Hulk's body to land on the other side. He finds himself standing between a pair of legs. He hears a rustle and the sound of something scampering along the walls. A cockroach?

He looks across the line of bodies. He can see the vague outlines of cloth bundles, stacked against the end of the passage. He can smell them—a musty, rotting smell that turns his stomach. He can't stay here for long. He is already short of breath.

—Dogs! How they sleep! Clutching their cocks. Deaf dogs!

He kicks at a shape in front of him. Its head rests on the curve of another shape next to it. He kicks again. The shape rolls over. He can see the face now. Sathi. The soda man is angry.

He bellows the young man's name. A sound like grating metal, calling a stubborn buffalo to its meal. He kicks at Sathi's leg. It takes many kicks to wake Sathi up.

He tries to open his eyes, but cannot. His eyelids are locked, stuck to each other. He tries again, but as soon as he opens them, they shut. Even the faint light is too much for them. He tries once more and sees a blur of hand in front of him. The light is cut off for a moment. A voice, tight with anger, rages.

—Up now! Out!

The soda man crosses over The Hulk's sleeping form once more, his hands firm on the walls. He goes out of the passage.

Sathi cannot lift himself up. His head is heavy and his eyes appear to be full of poster glue. He rubs them gently and feels scum on his fingers. He shakes his head until his eyes open.

He tries to sit up and get to his feet. One hand, wrapped around Natesan, has gone to sleep. He takes his other hand to it and picks it up like a piece of wood.

He stands up and finds his right foot trapped in the tear in his lungi. He pulls his lungi up and ties it round his waist. He can barely walk.

Insects have bitten him. Bed bugs. Lice. He must wash his clothes. Bathe. Should he wake up Natesan? He decides against it. Natesan likes to sleep. Anyway, he'll be up soon. He steps on The Hulk. The Hulk is lost to the world.

Once across, he holds on to the walls. Why did the old fart want him now? Kicking him up from deep sleep as if his house were on fire. Bastard can't sleep in his old age.

From the first day that Sathi had come to work, the soda man had pushed for it.

The soda man had a hard, rough face. A strong face. Someone had picked up a broken rope cot from somewhere for him to sit on. The cot was like a horse. Its legs split at the bottom and were held in place with a wire. The ropes had worn off and hung limp and sad. It was hard to tell the head from the foot of the cot. The soda man was too big for it. He sat in the middle, half his body falling through the thin ropes. His feet stuck in a mess of twisted rope. The boys sat at the foot of his throne-seat.

—So, Sathi. From Pasavur? Or a nearby village?
—Pasavur.
—Ever herded sheep or cows?
— . . .
—You must have. Only fields in Pasavur, nothing else to do. Know any farm work?
—No!
—So what? You can learn. I'll feed you every day, come and work on my farm.

Sathi did not answer. The soda man took his silence to mean that he could be pushed into farm work. That day, he hired him to work in his shop.

The soda man's farm had a large sheep pen. He was always happy to have an extra hand to graze the sheep and work around the farm. Earlier, untouchable boys could be forced into farm work. Being untouchables, they were happy merely to be able to live—eat a day's meal and be grateful for the new clothes they were handed out once a year.

But now, untouchable labour was scarce. They preferred to escape to the city and find any work there. Like Sathi.

Sathi loved the excitement of theatre work. Not for him the drudgery of the farm and the sheep. But the soda man never gave up. He tried his luck at least three times a week, pestering Sathi to leave the theatre for his farm.

Sathi walks out of the passage into bright light. The sharp morning sun attacks his eyes and he staggers. He walks past the booking room to the shops. He sees the soda man's cycle, with his food bag on the handlebar.

The theatre doors are open. Bare to the world. Like an exhausted man who can finally unbutton his shirt and relax, the theatre stands spent but happy.

The soda man is there, waiting for him, his elbow resting on the cycle seat. He looks impatient. He lifts one foot off the ground, then the other. Sathi feels irritated, just looking at him. When the soda man sees Sathi, his face lifts.

—What kind of a boy are you? One shout and you should be up! Not sleep like you're dead.

Sathi stops. He must wash his face. He can barely hear the soda man. Sleep pulls at his eyes and blocks his ears. He also does not want to hear what the soda man has to say. He hates this farm talk.

—Master, wait. Let me wash my face.

He walks towards the water tank. The place smells of dried piss. He goes to the tap that feeds the tank. The ground under the tap is filthy and sticky. He stands away from the tap, leans forward and opens it. Nothing. He looks inside the tank. Dry. He turns the tap shut. It screeches in protest.

Downcast, he walks back.

—No water? Wait.

The soda man goes inside and fetches a glass of water. It is just enough for him to wash his eyes. The man gives him another glass.

He drinks it. It is sweetened with cumin seeds. He feels the bile rise in his throat. He takes a huge gulp of water again, but this time swishes it around in his mouth. He spits it out and hands the glass back.

The soda man puts the glass away and locks his shop.

—All right, let's go. Where's your cycle?

Sathi does not know what to say.

—Come. Or do you prefer to drink that lousy tea and warm your bum? Come, come along. She is making idlis today. With chicken curry. Come, work and eat.

Sathi's head drops on his chest. He chews on his shirt collar.

—It won't be much work. You'll see. A few sheep you have to take out. A job fit for a king. They roam, you hang around. Laze. Come on, let's go.

— . . .

—That bastard Ravi who worked for me just ran away. Stole a hundred rupees and ran! Ungrateful wretch. I was good to him. Forget that bastard. You're different . . .

—No, master, I . . .

Sathi sees the man's hand go to this white moustache. He twirls it into place. There is anger in that mouth.

—What 'No, master'? I'm asking you to come and you refuse. Wasting time, hanging about and eating rubbish—is that what you like?

—Not like that. I want to buy clothes today . . .

—What clothes? Come with me. There's plenty at home—my son's old shirts.

—You go ahead, master. I'll come later.

—You dogs have it good here. That's why you don't care. When you come asking for work, you say you'll do this and you'll do that. After a few days you're done for. Spoilt. Don't want to do an honest day's work. You'd rather gulp that stinking curry and protta than drink a good farmer's gruel. Bastards! Get lost! Think I care?

Sathi holds on to the soda man's cycle. Sometimes he wonders if he should go. Herding sheep can't be all that bad. He doesn't mind clearing cow shit. But stay all day on the farm? Tied for life to the same work day after day?

The soda man gives up. He curses Sathi and prepares to go his way. Sathi looks at him, as if for the first time. A tall man in a big, loose shirt with thick white hair. He looks old and beaten as he pushes his cycle away.

Sathi feels pity. Should he run after him and get on the back of his cycle? Try a day's work? Why not? He continues to stare at the disappearing figure.

Then suddenly, he jumps up and sprints after the cycle.

—Master, master! Money for today.

The soda man stops, puts his hands into his pocket and hands Sathi a five-rupee note.

—Here. I'm sure you'll eat it up today. If you come and work on the farm, you can eat at home and save your soda money. What do you say?

Sathi remains silent. He puts the money away in his pocket.

—Open that gate.

Sathi is about to open the gate when he sees Natesan running towards the soda man.

—Master! screeches Natesan, like a hunted pig. —Money for today's food!

His lungi falling, he comes panting up to the soda man.

—What money? Think I print notes? Think it grows on my farm? Money, money! You owe me money. Get lost!

His anger at Sathi's stubborn silence falls on Natesan. He looks ready to beat him up.

—Master, cut it out of this week's pay.

—What pay? Nothing much left. You've borrowed most of it.

The soda man takes out his purse. He also holds the lease on the cycle stand. Natesan gets a weekly salary for minding the cycles and a commission on the soda. But it's not enough. He needs ganja too. The soda man hands him a two-rupee note.

—Please, master, two more!

The man turns away, ready to cycle past the gate. Sathi stands with his hands on the latch, he hasn't opened the gate.

—Open!

The soda man shouts.

Startled, Sathi lifts the latch. The soda man floats away. Natesan's anguished cries follow him, as he cycles down the mud road to his farm.

3

Can't bear being called a beggary dog

The theatre is full, but the crowd keeps coming. There are not many people near the shops. People buy their tickets and go straight in—everyone wants good seats. The sofa tickets go on sale first, the chair tickets next. Bench tickets last. The film on current show is popular. Hero M.G. Ramachandran—MGR, 'the revolutionary leader'—attracts everyone, especially the poor. Not surprising that the counter opens with sofa and chair tickets. There would be few takers for them otherwise.

The soda man has gone into town to refill his gas cylinder. His son, Muthu, is in charge of the shop. Muthu goes to school, class seven or eight, no one is sure. He isn't at the shop often. But whenever a new film comes to the theatre, he is there. He has a sharp tongue and is always surly.

—So, the heir is here.

—Here all right! Black-faced son of a . . .

The Hulk and Sathi are busy packing bottles of soda into the soda-bottle holders. Judging the crowd, Sathi packs a dozen in one and half a dozen in another. He usually hoists the holder with the dozen on to his shoulder and carries the smaller one in his hand. Best to take as much as you can. It isn't easy to come out for more.

The soda shop is long and narrow like a bus. In a corner is the soda machine. The gas cylinder is sunk into the ground next to it and a web of wires runs from the cylinder to the machine. It can take three bottles at a time. The bottles are put in their slots and the machine twirls them around, filling them with gas.

Muthu is busy turning the bottles around in the machine and stopping them with little marble balls. There is a wash tub near the door. A barrel sits beside it. Next to these is a cement water tank. Wooden crates lie opposite them, spilling out of the door to the outside. A narrow aisle runs through all this, just enough for a single person to move through.

—Sathi, fill these bottles!

Sathi picks up his packed holders and leaves them outside the shop. He takes the empty bottles that Muthu holds out and fills them at the tank. His hands work to a rhythm, filling the bottle, removing it, placing another under the tap.

—Father will be back soon? Before the interval?

The soda machine creaks as Muthu tops a bottle with a marble ball.

—Should be. Put these out before you go in.

The Hulk is already inside the theatre. Sathi picks up three bottles at a time, necks between his fingers, and stacks them in the crates outside. Four lines of bottles with a lot of soda and a bit of colour. He picks up his holders and is about to go into the theatre when Mani comes running from the betel-nut shop.

—Dai, dai, look! Muthamma the eunuch!

Sathi follows Mani's finger and sees Muthamma coming towards them.

A very tall man in a sari, with a garland of jasmine flowers in his hair. Bright plastic bangles, long hair that falls well below his shoulders. No blouse, but the sari is wrapped firmly around his chest.

Muthamma is so tall, you have to stand on your toes to look him in the eye. He owns a limestone kiln in Vairiyur and goes from town to town selling lime.

—Give me a colour soda.

As he puts the bottle to his mouth, Mani steals up from behind and pulls at his hair.

—Muthamma!

His voice is taunting. Muthamma turns around and fixes Mani with an angry stare. Mani retreats, then edges his way to her.

—*'Muthamma, my Muthamma . . .'*

He hums a popular tune, puts his hand out and fondles Muthamma's waist.

—Dog!

Muthamma snarls and hits out at him. He knocks back the rest of his soda in one gulp.

The betel-nut man hurries up.

—What, Muthamma? Come for your favourite hero? Never miss an MGR film, do you?

Muthamma takes out a small money bag tied with coloured string and pays Sathi.

—What do you expect? Who else should I watch? Who's the heroine in this one? Saroja Devi?

—Savitri.

—Bullshit! Savitri came in for just three films. And this one's not one of them.

—Of course, of course! The betel-nut man agrees hurriedly. —Come by later, won't you? A few minutes, by the bathroom . . .

—Hmm, hmm! If she wasn't here today, I'd have a few things to say to you. I'll tell her one of these days . . .

Muthamma flounces off and throws an elegant hand out at the betel-nut man's wife. She sits inside the shop, child on her lap.

—Muthamma! Muthamma!

Sathi and Mani mince behind Muthamma, swaying their hips.

He turns and spits at them. Then he rolls a betel-leaf and stuffs it in his mouth.

—Dai, Sathi! Why tease that thing?

The Hulk comes out of the theatre, laughing. He places his empty holder in a corner of the soda shop.

—Know what? Singaan went with Muthamma once . . .

—So? You go too, if you want!

Sathi cackles at The Hulk and goes into the theatre. He wants to sell at least a dozen bottles before the show starts.

—Soda! Colour soda!

Sathi's voice rings clearly through the bustle. Muthu has finished with the soda machine. He brings out a broken steel chair and places it outside the shop. He sits down and starts to eat a piece of sweet bread from the betel-nut man's shop. The betel-nut man lets him do this sometimes.

Muthu smells bondas frying in the tea shop. He goes in and takes one from a plateful near the grimy door. By the stove stands the tea-shop man, the big and sweaty hippopotamus, dipping egg rolls in flour and frying them.

—Eat, eat! Young chaps like you must eat! Don't be like your father. Take one more.

—Enough, Uncle.

Muthu puts his hands inside the pocket of his shorts and wipes the oil away. Then he returns to the soda shop.

Sathi is back. He places his empty holders inside, picks up a full one and goes into the theatre. There is still time. The film won't start for another ten minutes. He can sell more.

The Hulk comes into the shop, removes the empty bottles from his holder and starts packing in bottles from the crates that stand outside.

—Aiy! Don't do that. Go in and take your bottles.

The Hulk ignores Muthu's squeals, fills his holder and strolls away.

—Bastard!

Muthu mutters to himself and sits back on his chair.

—Muthu, dai! The cycle passes!

He hears Natesan's voice calling from outside the gate.

A sweaty and impatient crowd presses against the bars. Natesan is lost in the crowd. Muthu sees his waving hand and thrusts the packet of passes at him. The passes are numbered cards, made from cigarette packs. Natesan disappears.

Muthu sits back again. What a crowd! The second day of the new film and every show full so far. It should run for a while, this film. The crowds go wild when the songs come on. *'Dance on! Come, dance on!'* and *'O my new virgin book!'*—you can hardly hear the songs because of the whistles. No other theatre in the neighbourhood has an MGR film on.

The soda man wheels his bike in, the gas cylinder tied to its side. He looks sharply at Muthu.

—Finished turning the machine already?
—Uhh...

Muthu doesn't answer but goes out to help. They carry the cylinder inside and rest it against the wall. The soda man looks around him. He peers into the cement tank and yells.

—Dai! No water here! You'll need more water. Watch for the crowds tonight. I leave you alone for a few minutes and you waste time eating rubbish. Lazy dog! Work more and eat less! What the fuck were you doing all this time?

Muthu's face darkens with anger. He pouts and looks ready to cry.

—Why are you standing here? You bastards don't do anything and you get angry if I scold you. Move on! See if there's any water in the tank near the booking office. Go!

Muthu goes out reluctantly. The booking room is still open. He looks through it into the theatre. The credits are showing. He walks to the tank near the booking counter.

All around it, the ground is wet with piss. Muthu tiptoes his way, wary and disgusted. He finds the tap, opens it and water gushes out. He holds the pipe and jumps up on to the tank. It is almost full. The water is still, like a slab of slate. Polished. They must have filled it only a little while ago. Muthu looks at the water closely and sees a layer of bright green moss at the bottom of the tank.

He comes back to the shop and bails out the last bit of water from the cement tank into the washtub. Then he takes a brush and scrapes it clean. It is hard work—the tank is wide and deep, an old-time concrete one. Done, he throws the brush down, short of breath.

—What now, is there water? Or should we . . .

The soda man is impatient.

—No need, Pa. Full. But the booking office is still open.

—Go look! They'll finish soon. Sathi, go with him.

Sathi watches the booking-office people leave with their tickets and money box. Only Periasamy, the ticket assistant lingers. He should be gone soon. Soon enough, Periasamy switches the lights off in the booking room, shuts the door and leaves. Sathi watches, pretending to piss.

He is glad the booking counter tank is full. They would have to go to the nearest market town otherwise, to the bore-pump with the long piston. Not an easy thing to crank. And the soda man is never happy with one or two pots. Sathi takes two pots at a time on his cycle, sometimes he makes as many as ten trips. Usually, The Hulk comes along.

Thankfully, there will be no need for that today. Unless the manager catches them taking water from the booking counter tank. He is watchful, that one, suspects that they steal his water. Sathi knows the theatre watchman is on his side. He won't tell. In return, he helps himself to an occasional soda. In any case, no one but the manager minds. He should be busy for the next half an hour at least. Enough time.

Muthu brings The Hulk along and The Hulk and Sathi take a pot each. Muthu climbs on to the tank and Sathi hands him the pot. He fills it and hands it back. The soda man takes the pot from Sathi and pours it into the cement tank in the shop.

By the time we're done, thinks Sathi, half this tank will be empty.

Spotting them at the tank, the tea-shop man sends his helper, Vattan, along with two pots. They work silently and soon half the tank is empty.

Muthu calls out softly to Sathi.

—Dai, open the tap and let the water out.

—Why bother? We're done.

—Let the water out! If there's enough to drink in the tank, no one'll buy soda. I'm telling you, let the water out. Don't stand there like a deaf-mute. Come on!

— . . .

—You know nothing! Muthu is angry. —Leftovers-eating dog! Beggar! Do what I say!

Sathi's body shakes with rage and shame. His face turns black, the bottom of a coal bucket. He stands there, taut and burning. He usually doesn't mind insults. He brushes them away—useless words. But he can't bear being called a beggary dog. It makes him furious if someone taunts him with those words—mocks his life.

He stands there, fixed to the ground.

Muthu calls out angrily and asks for the pot. Sathi does not move. The Hulk returns with his pot and Muthu fills it. Sathi still does not move. The Hulk is puzzled. Sathi should have filled his pot and moved on. What is it? He shakes Sathi.

—What's up?

—I called him a leftovers-eating dog! Fellow's too proud. Can't take it! So he stands like a corpse. Dead dog!

Muthu replies from above the tank.

—Fucking swine! Who lives off leftovers? You and your father! Making money off dirty bottles. You'll get your ass whipped one day!

The Hulk yells at him.

—Oh, shut up! I know all about your Sathi. He was a down-and-out. I've seen him digging in the waste outside Jothi Hotel. Natesan found him and brought him here. Why get pissed if I say it now?

Muthu laughs for a long time, hooting while Sathi looks on.

Suddenly, with a strange throaty sound, Sathi throws his pot away, jumps up and punches Muthu. He gets him on the thigh. The sudden attack knocks Muthu off the tank. He falls head first into the smelly mess around the water tank.

—Dai, dai, Sathi! Enough! Don't forget he's the master's son. Let's go, dai . . .

The Hulk's words fall on stony ears. Sathi lifts Muthu up by his shirt and knocks him back into the filth once more. Muthu screams like a wounded dog.

4

The well is large and probably very deep

The walls are relieved and breathe easy. The thrumming applause has long ceased. The film is over. The excitement has died down and the piercing wolf whistles have stopped. Tired feet, glad not to be stood on any more, rest on the floor. The screen stares, clear, white and silent. All the theatre doors are wide open. They slam shut and open again in the happy fury of the wind.

Sathi and Natesan sit on the chairs. Sathi is full, content, as he sits staring at the screen. There is something he relishes about the emptiness.

Natesan leans back in his chair. Head on the edge of the headrest, legs raised and planted on the chair in front of him, level with his chest. His face is creased with exhaustion. Spit from his mouth has dried to a thin white line on his chin. His cheeks are unwashed, his skin oily. To Sathi, he seems deep in thought.

Above them, a ceiling fan swirls. A sparrow's nest hangs from a hole next to it. The birds fly about fearlessly, screeching. They wing their way from one side of the theatre to the other, their fragile bodies like tiny bales of loose thread. Their chirping falls on tired ears, glad for the music.

Natesan wakes up to their sounds. He turns to Sathi and holds out his hand.

—Give me a bidi.

Sathi searches in his shirt pocket. Nothing. He grimaces and shrugs.

—Fuck!

Natesan is irritated. He gets up and looks under his seat. He searches under two rows of chairs and returns with a handful of cigarette butts. He fishes for a matchbox in his pocket. Sathi finds one first and gives Natesan a light. He smokes one of the butts himself.

They are silent.

Sathi feels something in him melt and escape with the smoke. He lightens and blows rings in the air.

—Sathi, that big-assed bitch . . . is she here?

—Who? The cleaning woman? You're waiting for her—that's why you woke up?

—Shut the fuck up! Think I care? What is she, my favourite actress? Look at her. Got nothing but a bum.

Seen that fucking manager eyeing her? Rubbing against her with his silly grin.

—Is she alone? No husband?

—He's around. Married again, because they can't have kids.

—Hmm.

—She's not coming. Can't hang around here all afternoon. Seen the way old-goat soda man simpers when he sees her? Gives her soda free. He's going to put her on his lap and feed her with his own hands one day!

—Who cares! She's ugly, that one. Mouth's full of betel juice!

—I'll have her one day . . .

—Fucking boaster!

—Wait and see. You can come and watch. Want to hold up the lamp while we do it?

Sathi doesn't reply. He throws the cigarette butt away and bends down to search for another. Something glints at him from far away.

—Natesaa! A bottle!

Natesan clatters over the benches and chairs to the ladies' section. He finds it under a chair. Forlorn, half-empty, bottom chipped and dead flies floating inside. It looks like a drunk man.

Natesan grabs the bottle and shakes it. It gurgles. He stands on a bench and shakes it again.

—Sathi!

Only three of them sell soda inside the theatre: Sathi, Natesan and The Hulk. They sell fast during the interval. They must get rid of a couple of dozen bottles at least, for it to pay off. They need to move across the aisles, over the seats. There is no time to wait for customers to return bottles and pay. They come back later for that.

The lights go out when the end-of-interval bell rings and people push their way back to their seats. It's not easy to keep track of customers. Of course, some call out and hand them their money. But many forget, don't bother.

The soda man is strict. His sharp eye knows when something is missing. When the boys go back for a refill, he checks the soda-bottle holders and notes down every single missing bottle. No extras. The empty slot must remain empty, while the other bottles are refilled. That is his method of keeping track.

Not that it always works. The soda shop is often crowded and his attention is divided. It's easy to cheat him then. The boys manage to replace a lost bottle with a new one.

A bottle left behind!

Natesan fondles it like a puppy. He isn't tired now. The exhaustion has fallen off and his face glows with excitement. He saunters to his seat and puts his legs up on the chair in front of him. He dangles his legs, a triumphant dog who can't stop his tail from wagging.

—What, Sathi? Guilty eyes—must be your bottle.

—Piss off! If I open a bottle, I hang around till the fellow drinks it up. And I never forget a face. Not like you—one here for the bench types, one there for the chair types . . . and you don't remember anything at the end of it. Has to be you or The Hulk. It's you—probably doped out—that's why you don't remember.

—You've started that too! Next time you ask for the stuff . . .

—Oh, shut your face! Here, give it to me. I'll take it back. We'll talk to the soda man later.

Sathi holds out his hand for the bottle. Natesan moves it away.

—Get lost! The Hulk's right. You're a fool. I'm not returning anything. I'll sell it to the trash guy—two rupees I'll get.

Sathi and Natesan walk out. The bottle is hidden inside Natesan's lungi. The soda marble inside makes a rattling noise.

The tea shop is full of people drinking tea and eating snacks. Sathi's lips feel dry and he longs for a cup. But Natesan pulls him away.

—Forget tea! Come on!

The afternoon sun slashes his skin into bands of heat. The sun is high and half-hidden, a golden disc behind

Karatur Hill. Sathi smells rice cooking next door to the theatre. His stomach tightens. He decides he cannot walk for too long.

They reach their usual haunt—the abandoned market stall—and sit, leaning against its pillars. A lizard looks at them out of the corner of its eyes and clicks loudly. Natesan looks up at it, thick and flat on the ceiling. He remembers something.

—If my grandmother were here, she'd have brought us some food. She's gone. Probably staying away.

—Is she from here too?

Sathi is surprised.

—Kaanaan Street. She has a room there, but it's locked now. Back in a week, she said. She doesn't like staying with her son, so she's not with him. Wonder where she went . . .

—Father's mother?

—Mother's mother. How about yours?

— . . .

—What's the matter? Mother ran away with someone?

—Forget it!

Sathi gets up abruptly. He picks up a stone and throws it at a pig wallowing in a pit of filth on the road. He pulls up his dirty lungi and ties it tight around his waist.

—Want to go into the market? Might find some loose change somewhere.

—Don't feel like it.

—Let's go, just one round. We'll find something even if there's no cash—waste iron or something . . .

They walk around the dead market. Plastic bags, paper and rubbish swirl about in the emptiness. At the animal stalls, they pick up bits of iron that have fallen from the cattle pegs on the ground. Near the leather shops, Natesan finds a fifty-paise coin, green with moss and age.

Sathi's feet give way and he sits down in one of the stalls. His stomach is too far gone—it can't even rumble. He must never get up early. It makes him feel hungry like this. Getting up late, he can combine lunch and dinner into one big meal. He wishes he had drunk that tea. That would have quietened his stomach a bit. Natesan searches on, relentless in his hunt.

Sathi lies on his back and closes his eyes. The shadow is comforting. He drifts into sleep, until a sneeze wakes him.

He sits up and looks around him. Across the stall is an old figure, curled into itself, a dirty bag and a dirtier vessel by its side. Sathi stares at the creature for a long time. He curses inwardly and goes out into the sun once more.

—Natesaa . . . let's go—I'm so hungry. Enough, let's go. Can't take it any more.

—No problem, follow me.

They come on to the main road. On the other side, stand a few beef stalls and a row of small thatched houses. They cross over and walk through the narrow criss-crossing lanes that hold the houses and shops together. Soon they come to the new theatre that is being built. Rainbow Theatre.

Natesan walks into the construction site and goes straight to an empty warehouse of rusting iron pieces. There is no one there, only giant iron rods and slats. He returns in a few minutes, grinning hugely. His fingers clutch a dirty two-rupee note and a fifty-paise coin.

Beyond the theatre lie large fields and a few houses. Vairiyur. They walk through and past the fields towards thick shaded groves of coconut and palm trees. They turn into a grove, along a thin, winding path that ends in a squat hut surrounded by coconut trees.

The ground is soft and slushy. The trees were probably watered that morning. Outside the hut are clusters of men sitting on their haunches. Some hold glasses in their hands. A little away from the hut is a woman selling idlis.

Sathi and Natesan find a corner and sit down. Someone brings them two tall glasses. Coconut toddy. It smells delicious—freshly drawn. Sathi's mouth starts to water. He downs his glass in one huge gulp. Natesan sips slowly.

Sathi clears his throat and spits the gob of spittle out. He feels a shiver run through his body. He has drunk toddy before, but not recently. There is a strange taste in his mouth. He swallows hard and feels better. Natesan too has finished drinking.

They move over and sit in front of the idli-seller. She gives them a plate each. The sauce is thin, but spicy. They eat with relish, licking away at the plate.

Sathi burps and feels the taste of toddy go sour in his mouth. If he could have his way, he would lie down and go to sleep. Natesan is steadier on his feet. He walks briskly, almost running.

—Where now? Come, let's go back. Please, Natesaa...

—Back to the theatre? No chance. There's a well here, let's have a swim.

—You go. I don't know how to swim. I'll go back.

Natesan laughs loudly, as if he has heard a joke. Surprised, a garden lizard jumps off a bush and scampers up a tree. It looks at them, puzzled, its head on one side. Natesan throws a stone at it and it jumps to a higher branch.

Sathi looks at the tree. A big, cool neem. He wants to lie down in its large shade and go to sleep. Natesan starts to run, like a possessed man. In the distance is a well. Sathi follows him, reluctantly.

Natesan peels off his shirt and dives into the well. His lungi has slipped down while running. Sathi stands on the well's edge, feet planted away from its mouth and peeps in. A clump of small heads stare in amazement at the water where Natesan has jumped in.

He is suddenly frightened. What if Natesan doesn't come up? What if he's unconscious? He has drunk toddy.

The well is large and probably very deep. It is full with green water to the brim. A good, disused well.

A huge splash and Natesan comes up, clearing his lungs. Sathi breathes again. Natesan splashes in the water, a contented pup.

Sathi continues to stand at the edge. The other boys in the well, earlier startled by Natesan's dive, begin swimming noisily. They chase each other in circles, thrashing and jumping. Natesan looks up at Sathi and grins. How can he grin like that? Bugger! Sathi is annoyed.

Natesan pulls himself out, feet unsteady and hands shaking. He climbs out of the well and stands next to Sathi.

Another dive?

Before he knows it, Sathi's feet are off the ground and he flies into the well. Natesan has pushed him! Sathi feels his body rush into the water. Natesan jumps in after him. Sathi struggles to keep his head up. His hands beat the water, his legs kick underneath him. Mouth full of water, he splutters a curse. Natesan holds him by the hair and hauls him up.

5

His nose has been eaten away to a hollow

Sathivel lies on his stomach under the stairway, sleeping the sleep of centuries. His breath is even, like a gently whirring projector. His body is thick with dust brought in by the day's wind. So thick that it must be swept off with a broom. Saliva dribbles down from his slightly open mouth. Around him are lines of ants that have fled the heat outside. When he moves an arm or a leg, he crushes a few. Mostly, he lies still.

—Sathi . . . dai . . . Sathi, my child . . .

Heavy-toned, the voice drifts in clearly from far away and strikes his body. Sathi shivers. He feels himself melt in the warmth of that voice.

It is smooth and this makes him absurdly happy. He needs nothing, the voice is enough. It can break him down, make him do things. But he doubts if the affection that rides on that voice is real. It seems to wrap around him like a net, to trap him in an unguarded moment. He has to live with the fear. How does the voice scent him out?

The voice is near his ear now. Maybe it is a dream. He does not move, nor does he dare open his eyes. But it is no use. Sleep has left him. His hands want to strangle the throat that called out his name. But he also wants to rock himself and cry.

—Sathi, Sathi, my child . . .

It is not a dream. The voice is real. Unbroken in the wind that blows it in. He shakes himself awake and gets up quickly. He cannot make out where it comes from. He looks around. Nobody. Part of him wants to search out the owner of that voice. But he also wants to hide from it. He stands, undecided. The voice calls out again.

—Sathivelu . . . child . . .

The voice sounds hard and heavy with calling out. He can pretend he is not here, hide under the stairway. Then the voice will not find him. What if The Hulk or Mani or someone else hears and wants to know who it is? He can't let that happen. He gets up and comes out into the sun.

The voice is at the theatre gate. It has a slightly open mouth, like a water bird that pants with thirst in the midday sun. The voice has hands, held high over ageing eyes, blinking away the heat. The voice is a person—white hair hangs loose, covering his neck.

He wears a piece of dung-coloured cloth around his middle. His body shines in the heat. In one hand, he holds a dirty bag and a small filthy pot bound with cloth. Sathi looks at the man's fingers. They are more or less eaten away. The nails have disappeared.

He feels pity wash over him. He stares, tranced into sympathy. The man remains silent, expectant. The silence deepens and the voice insists again.

—Sathivelu . . . dai . . .

Sathi gives in. He is exhausted. He sighs loudly and walks towards the gate, wondering if anyone is around. No one, thankfully, either by the shops or by the theatre office. He stops halfway and replies softly.

—Pa, what are you shouting like this for? Can't you see the gate is locked? I have to come around. And please, don't fucking scream!

His father looks at him sharply through half-closed eyes. He is thrilled at being recognized, acknowledged. A wave of happiness breaks over his face.

Sathi is in no hurry. He walks over to the tea shop, asks for a cup of water and washes his face with it. He drinks a cup of tea. He looks for the old man—leaning on his staff, eyelids shrunk in the heat.

The old one walks around, looking this way and that for Sathi. He has moved past the gate. Maybe he thinks his son has run away, yet again, from him.

He must stop him before he reaches the tea shop. Sathi runs and catches him around the corner. He tugs at his elbow. He looks startled, and when he sees Sathi, lets out a delighted yell.

—Dai!

Sathi drags him firmly out of sight of the shops. The old man's legs falter, unable to keep pace with Sathi's stern march. They move on until they reach an empty plot, choked with thorny shrubs and bushes.

Sometimes a group of men shelter in the meagre shade the place offers and play cards all day. Today there is no one there. The stone on which the gamblers sit is quiet and still.

The old man lowers himself down on it, resting one hand on the ground to keep himself from falling. He is tired and it hurts to move an arm or a leg. He sits, his legs stretched out in front of him.

—Call yourself a father? How do you smell me out? No need to look like that. I'm not running away. Back in a minute.

Sathi walks back to the tea shop and asks for another cup. He covers it with his hands and returns to his thorny shelter.

He is scared—could anyone have seen him? His heart pounds inside him crazily. He pushes the glass of tea into his father's hands and asks him to drink.

The old man holds the cup carefully with both his hands, as if it were a lamp, and drinks.

—Why the fuck did you come here? To tell everyone, 'I'm Sathi's leper-father. I wander and beg for a living'?

—Dai, Sathi, don't talk like that. What can I do? Can I help it—maybe it's my fate. How can I not see you, you tell me that. You're all I have.

—Shut up! Don't talk crap to me. I can see how fatherly love comes out of your pores. God knows how you find me. You can't even bloody see!

—Do you think I send spies after you? The sparrow man told me you were here.

Sathi takes the empty cup back to the tea stall. His head aches. He doesn't know what to do with the old man.

Why can't the old dog die? Why must this demon-father pursue him like this?

It would have been better if he'd run away with a loose woman, like The Hulk's father had. How many times has he tried to get away from the old dog, but he still chases him. He must put an end to it this time.

There is simply no way around it. If the old bastard haunts him after this warning, he'll break his leg and throw him into one of the empty stalls in the market.

Wild imaginings crowd out sane thoughts as Sathi comes back to his father. Bidi smoke floats out of the thorny shelter.

—Why the fuck does he need a bidi? Sathi mutters to himself. —All right, now get lost!

The old man looks at him sharply.

—Bloody half-caste! Always denying me what I want! I'm your father!

—Want me to be proud of it? Look, don't come to the theatre saying you're my father. I'll only get sneered at. And that soda man won't keep me if he finds out I'm a leper's son.

—Don't say that. I know that man, he's not bad. I know him from before.

—Look, just get lost, will you? I've got work to do.

The old man unties his cloth-covered pot and holds it out to Sathi.

—Sathi, you know Keerthi from Aravur? A bit of beef from his house. I brought it for you. Not even touched it. Eat!

Sathi feels anger forcing its way up his throat. His voice, when it comes out, is breathless with fury.

—You old son of a bitch! You expect me to eat the stuff that you've begged for! Pack up and move on! Don't make me angry. Just go!

—Dai, Sathi, I'm telling you I've not touched it with these fingers! I'm sure you've not eaten well for days! Come, eat.

The old man's eyes are wet with tears. Sathi doesn't move. He stands away from the offering.

—Forget it! Just go now. Look, if you don't go, I will!
—Why must you shout like that, Sathi?
—Who's shouting? You're getting on my nerves now. Why can't you just fucking go?

The old man takes his pot back and ties it up carefully with the cloth. His hands shake but have not yet lost all their strength. The feet are different. Sathi cannot bear to look at them. The nose is worse, it has been eaten away to a hollow. The old man slings his pot back on his arm and gets up. He opens the string bag tied round his waist. It jingles lightly with coins. He pulls out a crumpled ten-rupee note, folded many times over.

—Dai, Sathi, at least keep this. Please don't say no.
—Oh ho, so you've earned this money for me?
—Keep it, Sathi. Buy a shirt for yourself. Come, take it!
—I don't want it. I have my own money, you keep yours.
—Take it for my sake. A father's gift.

Sathi snatches the note that hangs tight in the old man's grip and drops it into his own pocket. The old man looks happy. He starts walking. Sathi holds him back.

—Pa, I want this to stop. Today is all right, but don't ever come here again. What if I'm your son? If you want your son to be well, don't come around.
—Dai, Sathi, I've got you in my eyes. I can't help it. How can you ask me not to come?

—All right, all right, don't cry. You still sleep at the Vairiyur temple? I'll come and see you. You don't have to come after me any more.

—Will you really come?

—I will, I will. But not if you come here again. Then I'll disappear forever. Just run away, far away.

—No, no, don't do that. I won't come. You stay here. I'll go. But buy some clothes for yourself. Eat well. If you don't have money, come to me. I've given twenty rupees to the sparrow man. He's keeping it safe for me.

He moves away, leaning on his staff.

Sathi breathes a huge sigh. His head feels heavy. He must find Natesan and get hold of some ganja. He shakes his head hard and walks away.

6

Sathi kicks at the gate

In a few minutes the counters will open for the night show. There are crowds already at the gate. For a film such as this one, there is no need to worry. The seats fill up, even though it has been running for a week.

He drops the dirty soda bottles into the soap-filled washtub and lets them soak for a while. He cleans them one by one with a wire-bristled brush. As the brush twists inside, dirt and soap rise up in a grey foam to choke the bottle's neck. The brush shrieks against the glass as Sathi forces it. Then he dips each bottle in the clean water tub.

Sathi looks at the bottles with pride. They glow soft and shiny in the lamplight. The Hulk sits a little away, filling the clean bottles with water from the cement tank.

His hands move busily to their own rhythm and he talks all the while to the soda man.

—Then, master, that projector-operator, that Kajendran, he took a bottle of Torino. Said he'd pay you later.

—Fucker! Give me another one. He never pays me. He used to be happy with soda. Wants bottle drinks now, does he? Who the hell asked you to give him one? We'll never see the money. Guys like him hang around with their tongues out for a free drink. Give them the feeling we're fools and they'll queue up, cock in hand. Just waiting for a chance, these dogs! Try asking him to extend the interval—tell him we'd like to sell a bit more and see if he'll oblige then!

The soda man hisses angrily, popping a marble into a bottle. He turns the soda machine and it screeches as it fills the bottles with gas. The soda bubbles and flows over the stopper. One more round on the machine and the bottles are ready to be sold.

Sathi continues to wash. He is done with the plain soda bottles and starts with the coloured ones. The water in the washtub is greyish-yellow, the colour of wet cow dung. Sathi knows the master is angry and works silently. So does The Hulk.

A man rushes into the shop, his thin, high-pitched voice slicing the quiet of work. It is the theatre manager.

—Brother! He looks beseechingly at the soda man.
—Can you send across one of your boys? To let people

through the door? My man isn't here yet. Sent him to town—had to put up 'Last day, last show' posters. Please!

The soda man stops turning the machine. His voice crackles with rage.

—Oh, yes, I should send my boys when you want them! But when I ask for one of yours, you make a face and say no. If one of my boys hangs around inside the theatre, looking for custom, you send seven hundred men after him! Do boys come for free? I pay them a commission on everything they sell. And now you want my boys just like that. Fucking cheek!

—Brother, brother! What can I do? You know how it is. The boss decides all. Will he listen to me, a poor employee?

The manager sounds humble, but this makes the soda man rage more.

—Your boss! I know the type. I knew his father well. Man used to hawk clothes, carrying a bundle on his head from village to village. But today, today, your boss has cash in his pocket and with cash comes arrogance. He makes his own laws. Is he going to take less rent from us, if we help him out like this?

—Brother, you've got to help! Don't let me down now. The boss—think I respect him? The way he keeps calling me 'asshole'. No one will swallow such things, but I. What can I do? I've worked here for so long. Where'll I go?

—All right, all right, stop whining at me. I'll send someone.

The manager is in his usual faded trousers and shirt. He irons them. A thin, weedy man. Sathi wonders about his voice. For someone who looks so pale and miserable, it's pretty sharp. Especially when he barks orders.

The soda man sends Sathi to the manager. But he continues to mutter obscenities at the theatre owner.

Sathi goes out of the shop. The theatre bell rings. Ticket time.

—Go stand near the chair-side entrance. They'll come first.

Sathi does as he is told. He walks up to the chair-ticket entrance and opens the door. Not too many people. The line is long but they are not pushing to get in. People hand him their tickets. He tears the tickets in half, keeps a piece and hands them the other. They go in, one by one.

The film-reel man appears next to Sathi. He usually wears white trousers and a white shirt. But today he has on a lungi. He is from Malayur Thanmuga Films.

Every time one of their movies is shown, he comes along. Sometimes, theatre owners rent a set of movies from a distributor for a fixed price. Then, there is no need for an extra film-reel man. But when a theatre owner rents through a retailer, the man comes along as part of the deal. He gets a percentage of the day's earnings.

The film-reel man walks up and down the verandah. He sits for a few minutes on the stairs. Then gets up and goes to the shops. He comes back and waits by the stairway, looking at the people coming through the chair queue. He slips into the booking room.

The crowd continues to troop in. Some, who have come for bench and floor tickets, reluctantly pay the extra for chair seats. How long are they to wait for the bench and floor queue to open? What if they don't open at all?

The film-reel man comes out of the booking room towards Sathi. He nudges him aside. Sathi makes room for the man. He lets ten people in without asking for tickets. They have already paid at the booking counter, but they have not been given tickets. An arrangement between the booking-room clerk and the film-reel man. Who's to know?

But trouble breaks out soon. A pugnacious type pays at the counter and asks for his ticket. He is told that it is all right, he can go in. He protests.

—Dai! What bastards! Give me my ticket! Who's going to get caught if the ticket checker comes?

—Come on! Get a move on.

The film-reel man grabs the troublemaker by his collar and pushes him into the theatre. The man pushes back and stays out. Sathi raises his hand to grab him by the shoulder.

A few of the people who have been let in without tickets come out to stare in fear and amazement. The troublemaker edges Sathi's hand away with his elbow and stumbles into the theatre.

—Bastard!

A curse echoes inside.

The film-reel man moves in close to the booking counter and stands there. He makes a sign that only Sathi can see—finger on his mouth. Silence. He moves his head to one side and puts his right palm on his cheek. Sleep.

Sathi nods but says nothing. He looks away and waits, his face tense, for the next man in the queue to hand him his ticket, as if his entire life depended on it.

The floor and bench tickets are yet to be issued. The crowd continues to join the chair queue. The soda man comes in and calls out to Sathi.

—Come here for a minute! There's no one at the shop. Ask the film-reel man to stand in.

The film-reel man grimaces but comes to the door. He takes the torn halves of the tickets from Sathi. He does not want to stand there. Maybe he thinks it's too low-down a job. Not good enough for a film-reel man.

—Aiy, Sathi! Come back soon!

Sathi follows the soda man out. He gives Sathi ten rupees.

—Go get five bench tickets. Say I asked for them.

The booking clerk looks sharply at Sathi. His hangdog look disappears for a moment. His face crumples into a sneer.

—Get lost! Not again! Go stand in the queue.

Hearing him yell, the soda man comes in.

—What the fuck? Am I asking for free tickets? Next time you come to the shop and pick up a bottle of soda, I'll show you. Have you ever paid for one? One rule for you, another for me, ha? I've been here since this bloody theatre was built. You're nobody. Think you own the place—bastard! Look at this—a chap who comes in yesterday is telling me what's right and wrong . . .

—Aiy, aiy! Aiy, soda! Don't go mad. It's you, is it? If I'd known—here, take your tickets.

—You idiot! The booking clerk turns and whispers to Sathi, gritting his teeth. —Why didn't you tell me before?

The clerk opens a new ticket bundle and tears out five tickets for Sathi. Sathi's lips twitch. He gulps back his laughter, but his face shows a sly grin.

—Laughing at me? It's all your bloody fault! The booking clerk is sore.

—Sathi, go find that old bastard watchman. Tell him I want the outer gate keys. Take the keys from him and let those guys in through the main gate. See them?

The soda man points. A group of bare-chested men in lungis stand with their faces pressed to the queue door. Sathi strains his eyes to look and nods.

—Good. Let them in.

The soda man gestures to his friends to come to the main gate. Sathi goes towards the ladies' section. The crowd there is large and unruly. Women fall over each other, trying to get in. The old watchman blocks them at the entrance with a leg stretched out and one hand held high. He is a narrow arch of limbs. The women filter in, one at a time.

When Sathi gestures to him, the watchman does not react right away. He takes his time unrolling his waistband to take out a large bunch of keys. A mass of jangling iron tied to a big heavy ball. Sathi takes them from him. He almost drops the keys; they are that heavy.

—Dai, Sathi, careful, all right? And quick.

Sathi jogs to the main gate. There they are, waiting for him. But there is also a huge crowd waiting to get in at the main gate. At least a hundred people pressing against each other and the gate.

The gate is the kind that opens outwards. Sathi kicks at it, packing all his power into his right leg. Making sure that it stands tight against the crowd, he unlocks the gate and lifts its heavy latch. Then he opens it just enough to let one person in at a time. When the soda man's friends are all in, he pushes the latch into place and locks up. He hands them their halves of the tickets.

Sathi is short of breath and aching from the effort of holding the gate back. He stands, leaning against it. Maybe he should sit, for a while at least.

He feels for a bidi inside his shirt pocket and lights it. As the smoke fills his throat and enters his lungs, a warmth spreads over his chest and down into his stomach. He finds his strength returning.

Bidi in mouth, he double-locks the gate. He must get back to the watchman soon. Looking up, he sees the manager come towards him. He quickly whips the bidi out of this mouth and holds it behind his back.

Before he can say anything, he feels the sharp sting of a slap across his cheek. Like a snakebite. His feels his face go hot.

—What the fuck do you think you're doing? You should be at the chair queue. Not at the gate, letting people in as you please . . . asshole!

The manager doesn't wait for an answer. His fury still burning, he hurries towards the ladies' section to find the watchman.

Sathi rubs his cheek, takes a big puff from his bidi and flings it down. Keys jangling, he runs after the manager.

The manager is already there, haranguing the watchman in his shrill voice.

—Aiy, oldie! Lost your head or what? Some idiot asks you for the keys and you hand them over—now ten people have come in. Who's paying for them? You? Shall I cut your salary? Bloody careless fool. Who wants you here? If you can't work, just get the hell out!

—Not me, it's the soda man who . . .

—What bloody soda man? So you'll hand over the keys if he asks you? Tomorrow he'll want you to suck his cock. Will you? Dai, Sathi! What are you gawking at me for? Go and let people in. Go!

The women coming into the theatre stare coldly at the manager. The old watchman stands still, wearing a long-suffering look. When the manager subsides, he shakes his head.

The watchman is an ancient. With his sunken cheeks and lean face, he looks like a withered garden lizard. Sathi hands the keys to the old man and runs to the chair-ticket queue.

The film-reel man is furious.

—Where the hell were you? Took your time! Go help Periasamy—he's putting in extra chairs. He could do with a hand.

Periasamy is the oldest of the boys who work around the theatre. Dark-faced, with a bristling moustache and faded pants. Sometimes, he joins Sathi and the others in selling soda inside the theatre.

Sathi kicks at the gate

Sathi goes to the office room. A stack of chairs has been brought out of the office and lies waiting for him. Periasamy is inside, bringing out more chairs. From inside, he hears the manager yelling at the theatre's projector-operator.

—You! You're the operator! Why do you listen to these shopkeepers? Not more than five minutes—don't give them a longer interval just so they can sell their stuff. These chaps will ask for the moon if you let them. Why the hell do you listen to them? What things do they give you? Things to drink, eat? So, will you lick shit if they ask you to? Bastards! They'll be happy with an hour's interval!

Sathi sighs. Where does that manager find the energy to keep on like this? The operator, Kajendran, remains silent. In fact, Sathi can't remember the last time the man spoke.

Short and slight, no one sees him come in or go out. He flits in and out of the theatre like a shadow. He spends most of his time inside the cabin, never feels the need to come out, explore, find out about the world. The man seems content, somehow. He is often found in a state of half-dream. Sometimes, half-asleep, he forgets to push the carbon sheet in place.

One time, in a fit of self-forgetting, he got married. The woman died during her first pregnancy. Kajendran continues to work. He seems mechanical, a piece of half-animated wood.

Like the screen that suddenly bursts into life, he manages a smile sometimes.

After many days, or months, nobody knows, he found a woman. He was moved by a woman he saw at the theatre gate, crying and whimpering like a child. But this does not seem to have changed his life.

Sathi sees Kajendran hurry into his cabin. He picks up the chairs and goes into the theatre. The chair section is divided into two parts, with an aisle running between them. Periasamy takes the chairs from him and arranges them in the aisle space.

—Not bad, the crowd today, Sathi. Should all of us come in during the interval?

—I think so. No Natesan today. There's just The Hulk and me.

People keep coming in. Not a chair is empty. Even the extra chairs are being taken. No one on the bench and floor seats.

Noise fills the theatre. A lot of it.

—Brother, come here! I mean, here!

Some are using the towels they wear on their shoulders to reserve seats for their friends. Others object, whisking the towels away and sitting down righteously.

People kick the chairs out of their way, looking for place to sit. No one seems to want the extra chairs. Some

Sathi kicks at the gate

sit on them but soon get up. They look around, perhaps for a better seat and, finding none, sit down again.

An adventurous man picks his chair up and carries it to a spot he thinks is good and sets it down there. In the midst of all the chair-moving, a drunk picks up a chair and flings it away.

—Theatre! He yells. —You call this a theatre?

Periasamy moves fast and grabs the man by his shirt. He drags him to the office room. The drunk's lungi threatens to fall off. He tries to hold it tight against his waist.

—Let me go, you fool. Leave me!

Periasamy pushes him into the office room and asks Sathi to find the manager.

The manager rushes in and kicks the drunk. The man reels and falls down in a sad heap. His hands continue to play with his lungi. He fumbles, does not give up, fumbles again. The manager kicks him a second time. Lifting him up by his hair, he pushes him towards Periasamy.

—Throw the lout out of the theatre!

The drunk's face twists with pain. He grits his teeth. Periasamy drags him to the gate. Sathi is ready with the keys. He opens the gate and the drunk is pushed out. He does not go away, but kicks at the gate.

—Lout yourself! Dai, you've dared to hit me? Think you can get away? See if you continue to have your theatre tomorrow! Who the fuck do you think you are?

He continues to beat at the gate. He tries to pull it open. There are others waiting patiently to be let in. They move away.

The drunk's cries follow Sathi and Periasamy, who, by now, are far away from the gate and near the shops.

7

He whirls around, his hands held high

Matinee show time. The ticket counters are not yet open. The sky is white with heat. People huddle in the shade of the tea shop awning and the shadows cast by small thorny shrubs. They curse the theatre owner for not building sun shelters. The over-eager ones, though, are not fazed and hang on to the theatre gate. Unmindful of the heat, they wait patiently. Some squat on the ground and curse the sun. Many sit on their bicycles, waiting for Natesan, who is in charge of the cycle stand. Natesan is looking for Singaan. The waiting cyclists wonder if they should stand by the queue door instead. What if the tickets are all given out? They peer in the direction of the theatre office.

Natesan is at the tea shop. He lights a bidi and walks towards the cycle stand. He takes in the crowd outside the gate and by the cycle stand in a sweeping glance. A huge crowd, like at a temple festival. He hopes Singaan comes by. It is not easy to manage the cycle stand. And Sathi. He wants to find Sathi.

Taking his money bag and the cycle passes, he goes into the sunlight. Where is Sathi? Sleeping, most likely. He sleeps a lot, thinks Natesan. Should never have given him ganja. He's addicted now. A good beating might cure him, though.

He is not in his usual sleeping place inside the old sofa passage. Not under the stairway. Natesan peeps into the theatre. Not there either. He looks into the counter. He decides to climb up to the projector cabin. Halfway up the stairs, he sees him.

Sathi is curled into a ball on the small, square landing. Half his body lies in the sun. Sweat drips off his face. A line of small black ants crawls on his thigh. They go up and down, as if strolling on an empty highway. Natesan bends down and grips Sathi by his shoulder. Without a thought for his sleep, he shakes him awake. Sathi gets up, breathing heavily.

—Sathi! Get up! Enough of this sleep! How can you lie around all day like this? I'm going to the cycle stand to take stock. Big crowd today.

— . . .

—Come with me. Dai, can you hear me? Listen, go find the booking counter clerk. Ask for ten chair tickets. Say I asked for them, okay? Then come to the cycle stand.

Sleep clinging to his eyes, Sathi nods his head. He stands up slowly, holding on to the wall. It hurts to stand. His legs feel numb. Natesan is gone.

Sathi shakes his legs, rubs them. He looks out. Row upon row of heads below him. He wipes his face with the edge of his lungi and walks down to the ticket counter.

He sits in the verandah opposite the counter. It is cool. A breeze blows in from somewhere. He opens his mouth and shuts it. His throat feels dry. He needs water. The soda man has not yet come. The betel-nut shop is open, but the tea shop is closed. He has no choice but to go to the water tank. Walk through all that piss.

He is glad to find the tap has not run dry. He drinks palmfuls of water and splashes some on his face. How long, he asks himself. How long can I go on?

He returns to the verandah. The matinee show bell rings. They'll start giving out tickets now. He sees the ticket counter clerks come in, tickets and cash boxes in hand.

The chair-ticket clerk is not there. He works only during evening shows. Sunday is the only day he comes in for the matinee as well. His real job is at the post office. He hates it. Lousy pay, he claims. Which is why he comes to help out with the tickets at the theatre.

Sathi sees him at last. Panting, his body bathed in sweat, the postman-clerk shows up. He goes to sit inside his counter, looks at his ticket packets and rattles the change in his cash box.

—Sir, sir, ten tickets, sir. Natesan wants them.

He looks up at Sathi sharply.

—Get lost! Who does he think he is? Tell him the queue is already open, and no favours!

—Please, sir, this one time . . .

—Dai, when I say go, I mean go. Want me to call the manager?

Sathi is stung. The man must have already got a yelling from the manager. Or is expecting one.

Why the hell am I involved in all this, he wonders. Better find Natesan at the cycle stand and tell him.

He runs through the queue passage towards the outside door. Cautiously, he lifts the latch and the door opens to a thin line of light. The crowd outside pushes in, hearing the sound of the latch being lifted. Sathi presses his back to the door and pushes it out, just enough to let him through. But by now the crowd is upon him, ready to pour into the passage. He tries to find a pathway through the bodies. No use. He finds himself thrown back into the passage. The door opens fully and the crowd surges forward.

Sathi is in the middle of a vast sea of people. He flails his arms and legs, fighting the waves. He finds himself borne along on a raft of limbs. It is a relief when he is thrown out to land on the ground outside.

He picks himself up and walks to the cycle stand. Natesan has finished with one row. He drops a handwritten card on each of the cycles. The owner has to pay and return the card to Natesan before he is allowed to take his cycle out at the end of the show.

He is working through the second row. A sizeable crowd waits with their cycles for him to finish. It looks like there will be more than four rows today.

Singaan, another of the theatre boys, emerges from the bulging crowd of cycle owners. He wears a cheap sleeveless T-shirt. He rubs his chest up and down and stands in front of Sathi.

—The tickets?
—Asshole wouldn't give me any.
—Told Natesan?
—Not yet.
—Okay, I got a small job first. See that bunch? I'll go first. No, not in the queue. Outside, those guys waiting. See the chap in the yellow shirt? Go stand next to him. Looks like a good pick.

They push into the crowd of ticket buyers, slapping hands and bodies away. They join in the yelling and fighting. Sathi and Singaan move with the surge of the crowd, falling back or standing still as it demands.

Singaan is like a snake. He can slide in and out of any place, any crowd. He has long, strong limbs. His head is a knob, a smooth black blob at the end of a matchstick. He always wears sleeveless T-shirts. And a lungi which he ties high, almost on his stomach, showing his big thighs. He slaps them as he walks around, his bright eyes peering into everyone and everything.

After a while, Singaan slips out. Sathi sees him nod and leaves the crowd as well. Singaan flashes a bunch of rupee notes and thrusts a few in Sathi's hands.

—Go ask Natesan to get tickets.

Singaan disappears into the crowd again. Sathi stuffs the money into the pocket of his shorts and walks to the cycle stand. Natesan is almost done. Only a few cycles left.

—Dai! Couldn't get the tickets. Wouldn't give them to me.

—Finish this up. I'll go. Bastard of a postman. I know how to make him come around. Asshole!

Sathi takes over from Natesan. Natesan disappears into the queue passage. Just a few more cycles and then it's all done. The cycle owners waiting for their passes mutter and curse the heat. Only three left. They are impatient and excited.

Natesan returns before Sathi can start on the last line. He nods to Sathi and begins to move into the line himself. He whispers in a barely audible voice.

—Tickets? One-rupee ticket for two rupees! One-rupee ticket for two!

He knows there'll always be people to buy tickets for a higher price. The latecomers. Those who absolutely must catch the matinee show. All right, the passages are full now. But when the tickets run out at the counters, then . . .

Natesan hands five tickets to Sathi.

—Yours. Take charge. When Singaan comes by, give them to him. That postal clerk fellow was milk and honey. It all depends on how you talk, Sathi. You can't just push off when the chap says no. Got to hang around. All right, run. Don't forget—it's one-rupee tickets for two.

The crowd is a little thinner now. Sathi fans the tickets out like playing cards and calls to wavering bystanders. His eyes look for Singaan. Hard to find him in the crowd.

Singaan emerges from the chair queue and looks around, searching. His eyes catch Sathi and he walks over. He takes the tickets.

—Couldn't you have handed them over earlier?

—What? I just got them myself.

—Okay, see you later.

Sathi walks towards the shops. He feels light. Unburdened.

'If I can rule the world and if the world is mine to rule . . .'

He sings to himself, happy.

—There, there, that's him! I'm sure!

He looks up to see the man in the yellow shirt coming towards him.

The man grabs him by his collar.

—Dai! Where's my money?

Sathi tries to free himself.

—Take your hands off! Who the hell are you to touch me? He keeps an even voice.

—Dog! I don't even want to talk to you. I'll thrash you first and then . . .

The man tightens his hold on Sathi's collar. Sathi tries to push him away, but the man is strong.

—Singaan! Sathi calls into the crowd.

—What's this? What's going on here? Singaan comes out, bustling and serious.

—This chap stood next to us in the queue. Picked my friend's pocket—took everything. Yellow Shirt's friend pipes up.

—Hmm . . .

Singaan gently pulls Yellow Shirt's hands from Sathi's collar and turns Sathi around slowly.

—Him? This face? Are you sure?

—Sure. This was the guy. Kept bumping into me in the queue.

—But this lad helps with the cycles. Look carefully—is it him?

Singaan looks severe. The veins on his forehead stand out, tense. His lips press together. His moustache drips with sweat. Yellow Shirt sees that Singaan and Sathi know each other. His anger mounts. He roars in a voice thick with rage.

—Bastard! I know him. He's the thief!

The words are barely out of Yellow Shirt's mouth, when Singaan's leg lands on his jaw with a crack. He looks dazed and tries to hold his hand up before his face. A second kick lands on his right cheek. And then a third.

He falls to the ground, white-faced and frightened. Not to be outdone, Sathi kicks at Yellow Shirt's friend. The man falls down. He looks pleading, unsure why he has been beaten.

—Dai! Dai!

He calls out appealingly.

Singaan is not done with Yellow Shirt. He picks him up and shakes him. His huge hands grip the man's shoulders. Sathi hears a shirt tearing. Singaan is relentless. He pulls the man close to his chest and looks into his eyes.

—Dai, do you know this lad? Thief! You call him a thief? I'll break your chicken neck! Look at him—is he your man?

Yellow Shirt is speechless. He is almost in tears. His eyes clouded with fear, he stares at Singaan, stunned. His friend gets up and moves away, yelling.

—Dai! Bastards, let him go!

Singaan releases Yellow Shirt and pounces upon the other man. He kicks him down and punches him on his chest. The man squirms and wriggles, trying to free himself from Singaan's grip. Yellow Shirt, meanwhile, comes to life.

—Come on, let's get out!

He moves quickly, pulling at his friend's shirt. Singaan lets go and the two run madly.

Sathi puts two fingers into his mouth and blows out a series of sharp, triumphant whistles.

—Come here, you bastards! Anyone got the balls to fight?

Singaan is still furious and raring for a fight. Seeing that no one wants to take him on, he bites his tongue, lets out a huge breath and whirls around, his hands held high and his jaw thrust forward.

—Dai!

The crowd moves on, anxious to get into the queue passage. Singaan pushes his way through them, leaving Sathi silent and happy.

8

A lizard puts out a sly tongue

The interval is over and the crowd surges back into the theatre. The shops look ravaged. Their earlier quiet lies scattered around them. Empty soda bottles are strewn inside and outside the soda stall, as if tired and exhausted. They will remain that way for the night—things return to order only in the morning.

Sathivel has settled his accounts for the night. He sits by the stairway, a bidi dangling from his mouth. He puffs at it now and then. He is not sure if he should go on his own. Maybe he should take Natesan along with him. But the film-reel man might not like that. Maybe he shouldn't go at all. But he is curious, excited.

The film-reel man had called him aside.

—Sathi, after the interval, come to the room across the office. I'll be there. Just come and we'll have a little drink.

Don't tell anyone! Come quietly when the interval is over. What? Will you come?

Sathi can't resist the offer of a drink. He waits until the crowd has settled in and then slips into the theatre, as if he wants to watch the film. He waits a while in the darkened room and then lets himself out through the grill door that leads to the office.

The room opposite the office is closed. Maybe the man has locked himself in. Should he knock? He touches the tin door, it swings opens easily. He steps back. He feels his heart beat loudly in his ribs. He can't go in right away. He sits outside on the steps instead, his head on his knees. He is nervous, but he keeps still.

He feels a hand on his leg and looks up, startled.

—Come!

The film-reel man walks off. Now he has to go. He can't not go.

The door is half-open. He sees the film-reel man's face, beaded with sweat. He hesitates outside. The man stretches out a hand, pulls him in and shuts the door.

Yellow light from a fat, naked bulb floods the room. In a corner lies a heap of film posters and leaflets. A tattered mat in the middle of the room, with a half-finished bottle of whisky, soda and a glass. A pathetic old packet of chips lies on the floor. Two food parcels and a bottle of water are pushed against the wall. The stench of whisky is everywhere.

Sathi is unsure and embarrassed.

—Dai, sit down.

The film-reel man sits cross-legged on the floor. He is shirtless. Streams of sweat course down his bare chest. The room is airless, its window closed. The man pulls his lungi up to his knees and smiles. He looks relaxed, though he has drunk half a bottle of whisky.

Sathi sits across him. The film-reel man pours whisky into the empty glass and tops it with soda. He hands it to Sathi. Sathi has drunk toddy before, arrack too. But not this, though he has always wanted to. He feels the saliva build up in his mouth. His hesitation dissolves and he takes the glass into his trembling hands.

He looks up at the film-reel man. The man leans against the wall, his legs stretched lazily in front of him. He puffs furiously at a cigarette.

Sathi looks away and holds his glass tight with both hands. He raises it to his mouth, closes his eyes and swallows the whisky in one huge gulp.

Bile rises to his mouth. He splutters, clears his throat and puts the glass down. A pleasant chill shakes his body. The film-reel man holds out a handful of chips.

Sathi stuffs them into his mouth. The man picks up the bottle and holds it to his lips. He drinks and then pours a little more into the glass.

—No, brother! No, no, enough.

He does not listen to Sathivel and fills the glass. Sathi continues to munch on his chips.

—What, Sathi? How do you feel?

Sathi laughs. He feels both shy and full of shame.

—Nice, very nice.

His voice is small.

He stretches out against the other wall and draws his legs up underneath him. He sweats as the hazy warmth of the whisky spreads through his body. He opens the buttons of his shirt.

—Hot? Why don't you take off your shirt? That old bastard theatre owner refuses to put a fan in this room. Fucking son of a widow!

The film-reel man tips the bottle into his mouth once more. Sathi takes off his shirt, rolls it and keeps it safely beside him. He feels lighter, less sticky.

Black skin glows in yellow light. His body looks lit from within, his bones show through, shapely and beautiful.

Sathi is happy now, unafraid. The room becomes light and easy. He wants to clap and dance. Instead, he throws his head back and laughs.

The film-reel man looks at him intently.

—Dai, Sathi, ever drunk anything like this? Is it like ganja?

Sathi doesn't think so. Ganja lets him float more, makes him dreamy. But this isn't bad either. His tongue feels dry and he wants to drink some more. He smiles without replying.

—Sathi, your smile—it makes your face shine. Know why I called you? The others are all dogs, only good for clutching their cocks and sneering. That manager's a pussy! As for your boss . . .

Sathi laughs loudly. The film-reel man wipes the sweat off his chest and continues to talk. Sathi keeps laughing. He can't help it any more. The film-reel man's eyes widen in surprise, but he talks on.

—I tell that manager: 'What about that sweeper woman? Get her to come to you!' 'Why should I?' he says, 'Why should I? She sweeps the theatre every day'. He doesn't get a thing. Wonder if there's anything under his pants!

It is the film-reel man's turn to laugh. His mouth opens wide. Sathi notices that his hair is messy. He thinks the man's hair is like MGR the hero's, tousled like a sparrow's nest. The man's chest slides into a pleasing stomach.

Once again, the film-reel man holds the near-empty bottle to his mouth. Sathi's hands move, almost on their own, towards the glass.

—Go on, Sathi, go on! I like you, you know. Of all the boys, I like you the best. Know why? You don't talk much and you don't talk shit, that's why. You talk like this whisky. Warmly, softly . . .

Sathi gulps the last of his whisky down. The film-reel man shifts his body and moves closer to him. He pats Sathi on the shoulder. Sathi squirms. The man's touch feels wet and sticky.

—Sathi, do you know about me at all? What kind of a family I'm from? My grandfather was a landlord, acres and acres of land. Haven't seen any myself, but I've been told about it. My father. My father, do you know him? You must know of that bus service—the first on the Karatur–Malayur road. My father was a driver on that route. 'Motor-man', everyone called him . . .

Sathi feels deeply drowsy. He wants to laugh, but just cannot now. He controls himself and listens.

—And me! I'm just a film-reel man. Ten years, ten years I've been with Thanmuga Films. But just look at my life. Once I thought I would be a distributor myself, but I never found the cash. Know what it looks like now? Looks like I'll remain a film-reel man all my life!

The film-reel man cries loudly, his body shaking with grief. Sathi stirs awake. He holds the man's face up.

—Brother, brother!

The man closes his eyes. His head flops down and he continues to sob.

Sathi bends and wipes his tears. His feet nudge the empty whisky bottle and it falls over. He pushes it away to a corner. The man does not stop crying. He moves close, buries his face in Sathi's lap.

Sathi looks at the big whimpering figure with pity. His head has almost cleared.

—Brother, get up!

The film-reel man also tries to regain his senses. He holds Sathi's hands to his face and presses them to his eyes. Then he looks around, gets up and pulls the two unopened food parcels towards himself. He tears open the newspaper wrapping and flattens out the mess of food inside. Protta and kurma.

The man pushes a packet towards Sathi.

—Eat!

Sathi's stomach is on fire. He grabs a protta and tears at it. It is dry, and sticks to his teeth when he chews. He keeps eating.

Sathi hiccups. The film-reel man hands him a bottle of water.

—Sathi, know how long it's been since I ate at home? I miss my wife's cooking. Her lovely hands that push food at me as soon as I come home. Two months now. Two months. From Pasavur to Karatur . . . and from there I go, on and on, town after town. Never see my children, never see my home. You don't know what a miserable life I have. Lonely!

The kurma is not enough. But Sathi doesn't mind. He pours the last of it on his leaf and cleans it up with a bit of protta. The kurma is spicy and brings him to life.

—Sathi, my eyes are tired from not seeing my daughters. I just step into the house and they're on my lap shouting, 'Pa, Pa!' My eldest is in class five, the second in class three. How I miss them! Finish with one town and move to another. This village and then the next—not a single free day. Know what Thanmuga Films distributes? MGR movies. Boxes of them. Owner won't lease them. Wants me to take them around on a commission basis. And these films run! People flock in hundreds to watch them. Why, I don't know.

Sathi feels sorry for the man. Not a bad sort, but what a life! What can he do, though? He feels burdened by his own sympathy. He's not sure why the film-reel man is telling him all this.

I should throw open the room door, the theatre door and free the film-reel man. Free him and send him to his daughters.

Wild thoughts cloud Sathi's head. He feels angry, suddenly. He finishes his last bit of protta and licks the kurma off his fingers. He crumples the wrapping into a ball and flings it in the corner. He washes his hands with water from the bottle and pours some for the film-reel man to wash his.

Sathi tries to raise himself from the ground, but his head spins. He cannot stand up or walk just yet. He slumps back against the wall and watches a lizard put out a sly tongue to trap an insect buzzing by the bulb.

—Sathi, know anyone else who works like I do? And for what, I ask you? The shit they pay me—I can't even wipe my cock with it! Ok, forget it! It's my fate. Listen, know what happened two months ago? I went to my village—had an MGR film with me. After the show was over, I didn't even have time to go home. Sathi, I didn't get to see my wife, didn't get to kiss her even once . . .

The film-reel man buries his head in his hands once again and cries.

Sathi hesitates, then touches him gently.

—Brother!

Sathi takes hold of his hands and then holds his head to his chest. The film-reel man continues to sob.

—Brother, brother . . .

The man looks up from Sathi's chest and runs his hand over Sathi's face, tracing the curve of his jaw.

—Dai, Sathi. Believe me when I say this. I'm not lying, it's really true! Your face is just like my wife's. Same round face, soft cheeks. See, exactly like this. It's just the fuzz above your lip. She doesn't have that. You're so alike! Sathi, my love, Sathi, dai!

The man's voice pleads. His face is flushed.

Sathi leans against the wall. He cannot bear this intimacy. The film-reel man's hands go around Sathi's waist. His dark lips press themselves against Sathi's mouth. Sathi tries to free himself.

—Brother! brother!

He feels the man melting into him, senses an endless darkness take over the room.

9

The dice show nothing

The cycles are everywhere. Parked in hurried zigzag rows against the theatre wall and away from it in a wide, messy arc. From a distance, they look like the gnarled roots of an ageing tree. Between the first two rows sits a group of figures, gambling. Their heads are bent down to the game, only their shirts visible. Heads bob, squatting figures jump back and forth in excitement. Now and then, loud laughter cuts through the rows of bicycles.

An old woman passes the cot-shop outside the theatre and walks towards the cycle stand. She cradles a covered vessel in her hands. Her body is a curved hump and it is as if she is crawling rather than walking. She squints about her and finally finds what she wants. Natesan's face, mixed up with the cycles.

The old woman stops. She has to walk between the rows to get to Natesan. But which one?

She is uncertain. She must be quiet, she knows that. If Natesan sees her before she gets to him, he'll be angry, raise his voice, even a hand. She holds on to the cycles and creeps her way towards Natesan. She nears the gamblers.

—Five, I've rolled a five!

—Come on, put down fifty paise.

—Fuck! It's a two. Gone!

—Where's my one rupee?

Only two people are actually playing. The others are there to watch and bet on their favourite of the moment. The dice are cast on a mangled piece of rat-chewed cardboard. The goddess of victory smirks and stands by the man who rolls the largest number.

Singaan plays a weaver boy from Aravur. Sathi has a bet on. Fifty paise in favour of Singaan.

Natesan is not part of the gambling group. He is still busy with his cycles. He walks up and down, counting and making notes on a piece of paper. He has to account for all the small change in his bag. He will be busy for a while.

He sees the old woman and ducks between the rows.

—Natesu, aiy, Natesu . . . Her voice is thin.

When Natesan sees her walking towards the gamblers, he calls out to her.

—Grandmother, here!

Her shrunken eyes widen and she looks in the direction of the voice. She sees a blur. Natesan hangs his change bag on the handlebar of a cycle and walks up to her. He grabs the vessel from her hands. Surprised by the action, she stumbles. But she manages to steady herself and does not fall.

—Dirty dog! Grabbing like that! Always hurting me . . . rascal!

Natesan sits between the rows and opens the vessel. The old woman huddles into the shadow cast by the parked cycles. There is rice and thin tamarind gruel. The gruel is oily, flecked with bits of onion and coriander leaves. Natesan holds the vessel to his face and drinks up the gruel hungrily. A mess of rice, spiced with dregs of gruel sits at the bottom.

—You call this food? Tastes like sewage.

—You get what you deserve. Do you bring home chests of money?

The old woman chews her words and spits them out. To understand her, you have to watch her lips.

Natesan puts the vessel down and looks at the group of gamblers. Their bodies glisten with sweat and they are lost in their betting.

—Sathi! Aiy, Sathi!

Natesan calls out softly at first, then raises his voice. Sathi's head springs into view.

—What?

He looks up, clearly irritated, then turns back to the game. He is happy when the dice roll out and sad when they close in and show a two.

Sometimes, the dice show nothing and then there is high excitement.

Singaan sits back on his haunches, cradles the dice in his hands and throws them on the cardboard.

—Ha, ha! A twelve for sure!

Sathi's heart beats fast. He is relieved when he sees it really is a twelve. He hears Natesan calling him again. He doesn't want to go, but he gets up at the end of the throw and walks across. Singaan watches him leave, but says nothing and continues to roll.

Natesan gathers clumps of rice from the bottom of the vessel in his hand and stuffs them into his mouth. The liquid runs down his hands and back into the vessel.

—Come, sit!

He heaps a mound of drippy rice on to the lid of the vessel and hands it to Sathi. Sathi is tempted, but hesitates. The game calls to him.

—You eat. Don't feel like it. You called me for this, when I was busy playing? Sathi looks sulky.

—Dai, sit! Bloody game! Play it any time.

—Eat a bit, love.

The old lady whines. Sathi looks at the bent figure.

The dice show nothing

Face covered with fine wrinkles. Mouth that moves on its own, a piece of soft rubber. It opens and shuts, opens and shuts, unable to stay still for a moment. Her eyes are almost closed as she squints against the afternoon sun. Her voice reaches the outside from somewhere very far away. When she speaks, it is almost a shock. Her body is a fit home for a clinging bat to perch on.

—Nice . . .

Sathi reaches for his second handful.

Natesan glares at him. Sathi finishes his share. Natesan hands him the vessel, a bit of thin gruel swirling in the bottom.

Sathi puts the lid on the ground. Its edges are softened, bent with age and ill use. He takes the vessel from Natesan with both hands and drinks up the gruel. He burps, fits the lid on to the vessel and puts it down. The lid falls off. He beats it into fitting the vessel and hands it back to the old woman.

Sathi and Natesan need to wash their hands. They walk across to the rickety cot-shop opposite the cycle stand for water. The old woman follows them.

—Natesu . . . give me some money, please. Nothing at home.

—Shut up! You always do this! Where do I have money?

—Ask your master. Take an advance. Natesu, what'll I eat? There's nothing to cook at home.

—Why cook? Why eat? Get lost!

—You louse! Can't you give your grandmother something? You have money to spend on dust and drink, but not for me!

The cot-shop woman comes out and stands by her.

The old woman grabs Natesan's hands and pleads. He pulls away. He digs into his pocket and comes up with a handful of half-smoked bidis and some small change.

—Look, this is all I have now. Why the hell did you come here? Can't you just sit quietly at home with your son?

—Dai, dai, Natesu, ask your master? Go on, get me some money, please!

Natesan tries to free himself from her, but she gets her hands on him again and again. When he moves, she moves with him, almost falling down. He doesn't bother, pushes her away, freeing himself from her grip.

The old woman refuses to let go and each time he tries to throw her off, she staggers. The knot of hair, tight as a marble, at the back of her head unravels. Her mouth continues to plead.

Sathi shudders, watching her slight body sway this way and that. He looks at Natesan with anger and contempt. He wants to break his head.

With a great effort, he pushes Natesan away and takes the old woman's hand. Her hand is soft, slack and wasted.

He feels he could snap it with a tight grip. He takes a five-rupee note from his pocket and gives it to her.

The old woman takes it without a word and hobbles away to sit next to the cot-shop woman. She twists her hair back into a marble knot.

—Dai, Sathi, what are you up to? The old one's a sly thing. She's pretending. I'm sure she gets enough out of her son. Probably just hides it away, the old snake.

—Appappapah! So, I have a millionaire son? And he showers gifts on my head? Sure, come around and see my loft full of treasures. Pah! It's easier to dig a mountain to catch a rat than to get ten paise out of you. And you talk about my son!

She pauses briefly, looking around at everyone.

—Look, can't you speak to that manager and sneak me in. I'd love to see a film!

—Bad enough you managed to get money out of Sathi. Now you want to see a film! Get up and go! Don't hang around here. I don't ever want to see you again. Just disappear!

—Dai, dai, watch your tongue! How I carried you on my shoulders when you were small! How I looked after you! And now, even now, I go hungry to bring you food! Ungrateful dog!

The old woman points accusingly, beats herself and starts to cry. Dry-eyed but furious, she wails, screeching at Natesan.

Sathi wants to hug her, hold her to him and console her. He wants to punch Natesan in the face. But there is a man coming towards them and Sathi holds back.

The old woman continues to moan and curse, her frail body stubborn with anger.

—Five rupees, what'll I do with five miserable rupees? Things cost these days . . . such prices! What do you know? You would if you had any brains in that head of yours! When that bitch died, you should have died with her. You lived and now you talk like this! My fate, that a swine like you should abuse me!

The stranger looks perplexed. He asks in an uncertain voice:

—Cycle. Who's in charge?

—Why? Returns Sathi.

The old woman simmers down.

—Couldn't get tickets for the current show. I want to take my cycle out.

—How can I take just your cycle out? Everything's a mess. Come when the show's over.

Natesan sounds firm and hard. There is no sympathy in his voice.

—Brother, you don't have to do anything. Just come with me. I'll take it out myself and help you put the others back in. I've a long way to go. Thought I'd get tickets— MGR film, so I wanted to see it badly. But now . . .

—No!

Sathi gets up and leads the man a little farther away. He whispers into his ear. The man nods.

A minute later, Sathi is back, with a fresh two-rupee note.

—Natesaa... poor chap... give him his cycle. He has to go far.

—You go do it if you want!

Sathi ignores Natesan's anger and walks to the cycle stand. The man follows him. His cycle is in the third row, only ten cycles to move. He takes it out and puts the others back.

Sathi's ears register a faint shout. The sound of dice. It alternates with the fainter sounds from inside the theatre.

He returns and gives the two-rupee note to the old woman. He sits on the edge of the cot-shop.

The old woman's face is wreathed in smiles. She looks up at Sathivel. She strokes the sides of his face with both her hands and cracks her knuckles against her head to ward off the evil eye.

—Good boy! Come to my house. I'll cook a nice curry for you, with real meat in it. You can eat only if you have money! This dog doesn't understand that. Come! Will you come this week?

—All right.

—Aiy, Sathi, don't flatter the old thing.

—Shut the fuck up, will you?

Sathi flings his words at Natesan, who is busy counting his money. He is already calculating the price of half a kilo of meat. Maybe not tomorrow, but one day, he must visit the old woman and get her to cook.

—Is Singaan there?

The cot-shop woman's question breaks his thoughts.

—There? Yes, he's there.

—Natesu, listen now. I have to tell you this. You're like my own son. Please help me. I'll even fall at your feet if you want.

Natesan stops counting and looks up at the cot-shop woman.

Her eyes are full of tears. Her face is twisted in fear and she looks ready to fall at his feet.

—What's this all about?

—How can I even say it? Day before yesterday, that Singaan came and knocked at my door. Dead of night! I didn't know what to do. Couldn't even open the latch. I was that scared!

—What did he want?

—Said he wanted to eat a bridegroom's dinner . . . what does he mean, talking like that? There are places to go for dogs like him. Does he think I'm like that slut Karuvachi? That I open my doors to men at any time of the night? Leftovers-eating dog! Hope his feet get eaten away! Hope his hands fall off!

The dice show nothing

The cot-shop woman curses loudly.

—I only have her, she's grown up now, my daughter. I'm so afraid for her—must marry her off soon. After that, what do I care? But till then you've got to be careful. Like carrying hot coal inside your sari—it can burn any time. Then, everything will burn. Her honour, my shame . . . they come for her, the dogs, they scent her out . . .

—Oh ho, so that's what it is. Shall I come tonight? How much do you charge?

Natesan's humour is merciless.

The cot-shop woman bursts out.

—Taunting me, are you? May the worms eat that dirty tongue of yours. I'll kill her, push her into the well, before I hand her over to the likes of you. What do you think I am? My husband's been dead now for how many years? But have I gone to another man? You must be full of your dirty smoke to talk like this. Wretch! Dog! I'm telling you I was scared and you! Think I have no one for support? There are many who can help me. I just had to call and they'd have come running. That would have been the end of that Singaan. No Singaan left, just a pile of bones. But I didn't do that. Why? Because then, my girl's name would be mud, that's why!

The strength of her anger burns in her voice. Natesan stares at her. Sathi feels his breath become hot in his nose.

—Dai, Natesa, go on. You can tell that dog to behave. If he thinks he can get my girl like that, tell him to forget it.

Cut that thought out now, cut it at its root. I can't tell him. But you can.

—Motherfucker! All right, I'll deal with him. You should have told me earlier! I'd have given it to him. Shit-eating dog!

Natesan flings his change bag on the cot-shop woman's bed and walks off towards the cycles. Sathi follows him.

10

His voice booms and echoes off the theatre walls

Now Showing
at
Karatur Sri Vimala Theatre

The posters smell fresh and clean. Long narrow posters that have to be stuck in rows. Posters with bold, glowing letters on them. They lie in a heap outside the office room. Outside, a small fire crackles with wood from the Ashoka tree. A pot of glue sits on the fire. The theatre boys separate the posters and fold them into neat rectangles. Vattan feeds the fire. Sanmugan, who helps with the posters, is also there. He stirs the pot now and then.

Sathi's beat is Aathur Road. It is a bad place to be, but Sathi doesn't mind. Tappers work all night off Aathur

Road, bringing down fresh toddy from tall palms dotting the landscape. He usually manages to get at least a glassful of toddy for himself.

Gluing posters all along the long road is hard work, and when he's done, his bones ache for sleep. A bit of toddy helps along. He returns drunk and dead to the world, to go straight to sleep. Even in the days when he worked at Meenal Theatre, he always asked for Aathur Road.

Vattan usually takes over the town. He carries bamboo ladders, to stick posters high up on the walls. Natesan takes Pasavur Road. Mani goes to Malayur Road and Ganesan to Vetoor Road. Their usual beat. That never changes.

It is The Hulk who is the problem. He keeps changing his beat with each film. He always has an excuse, a reason, and the manager gets irritated.

—Out! Who wants you? Don't step into this theatre again! I'll break your bones if you do!

—No, sir! Please, sir! You don't know the problems, sir. If it's an MGR poster, every rascal in town wants one. If I don't give them one, they refuse to let me stick it on the walls. And if I were to give them all away, there would be no posters left to stick, sir!

The Hulk is right, though. MGR film posters are the rage. But he has an excuse for every road.

Asked to go to Pasavur, he says—There? Not me, sir. Dogs everywhere. I'll get bitten to death!

He laughs at his own explanation. The manager turns away. The others are tired of his stories. Mostly, he does what he wants to do.

The poster routes are well marked out: all along the Aathur Road to Thatoor and on Pasavur Road, up to Esaiyoor. Each set of posters is folded, then hung on the crossbar of a cycle. The better ones are kept separately in the carrier. Each bicycle has a plastic bucket of glue dangling from its handlebar.

The ageing watchman sits on the office steps and watches them get ready. He chews a huge wad of tobacco. He doesn't chew betel leaves, but his right cheek is always swollen with tobacco. Occasionally, he smokes a bidi, but then only Ganesh bidis. He has also been seen taking a secret puff from Natesan's ganja joint. But he says he prefers his tobacco. Ganja does not give him the high that tobacco does.

He loves it when the boys are together. His cheek dimples and his eyes fill with joy. Now, watching them at work, swiftly folding the posters, he is charged and wants to talk.

—Dai, did you all know that Rainbow Theatre is nearly built?

—So what, Grandpa? If they give us work, we'll go there. Natesan looks up from his work.

Sathi opens up a poster he has just folded and refolds it. The old man crooks a finger at them.

—Nnnnn. Nnn . . .

His sunken cheeks and thin bones tell a tale of their own. His mouth tightens up as he purses his lips. He looks like an excited child who knows something that the others don't.

—Did you know that you can't sell soda inside that theatre? Or biscuits? Or even tea and coffee? The owner's going to allow shops only if they agree to that. Only outside!

—All that won't work. If you don't sell inside, you don't make money. Think the women will come out and buy stuff? And if they don't buy, no business, Grandpa.

The Hulk's small eyes shrink deeper into his plump cheeks, as he wags a finger in the old man's face.

The old man is not cowed.

—What do you know? Nothing! Did you all know what your theatre owner, Minukkan, did to prevent that new theatre from coming up? Wrote to the government saying, 'There's no road to the new place. How'll people come and go?' That's why it took so long to come up. Else it would have been up in a minute. What's the use, anyway? Minukkan kept writing something or the other, but nothing happened. That fellow, the one who's building Rainbow—that flower-seller, flower-power—he's a smart one. Knows how to make a garland out of nothing. He somehow spoke to this one and that one in the government, and in three months' time, you'll have a new theatre. Wait and see, that'll be the end of our Vimala!

—He can do fuck all, that flower-seller. Vimala will have its crowds. When this theatre was built, what did everyone say? 'What a bad place! Sound system doesn't work! That's not right, this is bad . . . looks like a grain godown.' But look now. We have our crowds.

—Maybe, maybe. Aiy, Hulk, some say this was meant to be a godown. Did you boys know that?

The old man looks about him, in the direction of the office, at the shops. He curls his small body into an even smaller ball and his voice hums with secrecy.

—That Minukkan has two children. The eldest, they call Sadaiyan. He's a big shot in the ruling party. You all know the younger fellow, Singaram—leading light of the opposition. Old man Minukkan is an A.Aa.K. man. This Sadaiyan's wife—do you know her?—this godown became a theatre because of her. Minukkan was really rich then—had his own weaving mill. Had a car and a driver even then. He was planning to build a grain godown.

One day, he sees his daughter-in-law, Sadaiyan's wife, dressing up to go out. Looking at her, you wouldn't say she's from his caste. Fair and round, like a ripe tomato. Minukkan couldn't bear to see this red tomato going around like that—powder on her face, nice clothes . . . Before he knew what he was doing, he blurted out: 'What's all this dressing up? Like some cheap night dancer?' They say she got really angry. So angry that she yelled back, forgetting his age: 'I'm going to see a film. Know what a cinema theatre is? Ever been inside one?'

The old man stops to catch his breath. He peels away a bit of tobacco from a roll hidden in his waistband and stuffs it in his mouth. The glue pot is off the fire. With bits of glue sticking to his body, Vattan comes and sits near the old man. There is silence all around, only the rustling sound of hands moving over posters. Who doesn't love a tale?

—They say Minukkan was aghast. 'How dare she? How dare? Marries into my family, marries my son and then taunts me!' He felt so slighted that he decided then and there to convert his grain godown into a theatre. Just to show her. That's how this Vimala Theatre came to be.

—Who gave it the name Vimala, Grandpa? Was it the daughter-in-law's name?

Sathi laughs.

—Appappah! What kind of a laugh is that? You and your wide mouth! As if the old man would name it after a daughter-in-law. No chance. He had a mistress in Madaiyoor. Her name was Vimala. Actually, they say this theatre was her idea. She saw Minukkan upset about all this and gave him the solution. And he gave this theatre her name!

—I've heard a different story. That he quarrelled with the owner of Amaraan Theatre?

The old man gets up to spit. He goes to the shrivelled Ashoka tree and clears his throat. Red tobacco spittle falls to the ground. He returns to his seat on the steps.

—Give me a bidi.

Sathi removes the bidi stuck behind his ear and hands it to the old man. The watchman puts it to his lips, cups his hands around the bidi and strikes a match. He draws the smoke in deep, until it reaches his eyes.

The boys are eager, impatient. They wait for him to take one more puff.

He takes another deep drag of the smouldering bidi, sits back and then blows smoke into the air. The bidi is almost burnt out. He throws it away and resumes his tale.

—Back then, Amaraan Talkies was very famous. Such crowds! You know that petrol pump in Kanuru? It was near there. A big tent theatre, they ran it for many, many years. The fellow who owned it also ran another tent theatre. Koovalan, it was called. Near Kaiyuru. Know that MGR film, the one in which he is always doing good? Well, he'd start running it in one theatre and as soon as the first spool was over, he'd take it over to the other and start there too. So he'd have two shows going with one film! He kept an autorickshaw running between the two theatres to carry the spools back and forth. And the crowds! Both theatres always full. Fellow made a lot of money—ran his theatres well. So good, so good. No one has since . . .

The old man is lost in a distant memory. If he gets the chance, he'll talk on until he's short of breath. It is not easy to stop him once he gets his teeth into a good piece of story. Sathi cuts his rambling short.

—Grandpa, why did he and Minukkan fight?

Seeing everyone's eyes fixed on him, the old man decides to relax. He takes his undershirt off and fans himself with it.

—Hot. Too hot!

Sathi persists.

—Grandpa!

—You! The fellow would never have fought if he'd been from the same caste. But the Amaraan owner was from another caste. They were friends once—both had cotton mills, weavers working for them. In fact, Minukkan used to call him: 'My Friend'. And that man would say: 'Yes, sir.' But something went wrong, don't know exactly what. One day, Minukkan says to him: 'What kind of a man are you? Are you really running a cinema theatre or something else? You've got a tent and I'm sure you have dancing women in there. That's how you make your money.' Minukkan didn't know what he was talking about. Thought that a tent theatre was like a show tent with dancing women.

—So what you're saying is, until he built this theatre, Minukkan knew nothing about cinema?

Everyone laughs at Sathi's question. Even now, whenever Minukkan comes to the theatre, the boys laugh behind his back. Minukkan curses everyone he sees.

—Foul asshole!

His sons look after his other businesses, but he is in charge of the theatre. He comes occasionally in a car, stays briefly and then goes back. But when he is there, his voice booms and echoes off the theatre walls.

The old man continues.

—Minukkan has never seen a single film fully. You know that bit we run after the morning show interval—that one-minute track of the naked woman and the man squeezing her tits? That's the only thing Minukkan has ever watched. Stands in a corner and watches. I've seen it with my own eyes and I've been here for the past four or five years.

—Grandpa, what did that Amaraan Theatre owner say to him when he . . .

—Oh that! That fellow is a smart one, never said anything. Just sniggered behind Minukkan's bum! He kept asking Minukkan: 'What'd you say? Say it once more!' And Minukkan would innocently repeat his thing about the dancing girls and the fellow would laugh. And others too. Whoever was there would laugh at Minukkan.

Minukkan didn't get it at first. 'What the shit did I say? Why's everyone laughing?' One day, he decided to ask his son. He too started laughing. Minukkan demanded an explanation and when his son told him, he felt silly. 'That bloody so-and-so! Making a fool of me in front of everyone. I'll show him.' They say he was so angry that he decided to build his own theatre. Just to show him.

The boys laugh. Vattan and Sanmugan get up. It's almost time to leave. They pick up a bunch of old buckets standing in a corner and start to fill them with glue. The glue is not hot any more. But the boys are in no hurry. They have finished folding the posters, but no one seems to want to get up.

—Grandpa, we'll never know the truth.

—Sathi, you should've seen the theatre when it was first built. Bursting with people. Ticket counters working overtime. Sometimes Minukkan sat outside the gate on a small stool and gave out tickets himself. A chap would come up to him and say: 'Sir, I have only fifty paise.' Minukkan would frown, but let him in. He loved the sound of coins clinking in his shirt pocket. Those days, he looked good. Round and strong, like a nice piece of wood. Now, of course, he looks a bit down.

The manager is at the gate. He comes in, wheeling his cycle. Behind him comes the betel-nut man's wife, child in hand. The boys jump up and scatter to do their tasks. They fill the remaining buckets, bundle up the posters and put out the fire. The child holds its hands out to Sathi, but he takes no notice of it. He has to go. The old man gets up and goes to his corner.

—What? Finished? Ready?

The manager raises an eyebrow, looking severe. The boys shake their heads. Sathi goes up to him.

—What?

—Sir, give me five rupees, sir. Just an advance. Cut it from tomorrow's pay.

—Bastard, forget it. I've already given you a five-rupee advance.

—But sir, it's all gone. I had to pay the cycle-hire shop.

The manager shakes Sathi's hand off and walks on. Sathi runs after him.

—Sir, you know how far Aathur Road is. I can't go on all night. I've got to have a cup of tea at least. Sir, just five rupees sir, please. Take it from my pay tomorrow.

—Look, I'm done. Get lost.

Sathi continues to plead till the manager goes to his cabin and shuts the door.

No use. He comes back, his face small and lost.

—What? Begging for money? That son-of-a-whore won't give?

The Hulk has a smirk on his face.

—Dai! Watch it! Who are you calling a beggar?

—You! What about your father? A merchant, is he? Bloody beggar!

—And your mother's a runaway whore!

—He came for you that day: 'Sathi, Sathi, my child.' You weren't there. I sent him away. I know your leper-father.

Sathi clenches his fists. His heart shrinks to a small point within his ribs. His body feels hot with shame. He bends down, picks up the pile of posters and walks towards his cycle.

The Hulk's laugh follows him.

11

He feels sapped and flops back into his seat

The ticket counters are open. Not too many people. A few chair tickets have been taken and some bench ones. The floor tickets are yet to be issued—the floor seats are still empty.

Sathivel enters the theatre with his soda-bottle holder. He looks around and decides to wait for a while. He puts the holder down and sits on one of the chairs. A thin breeze plays on his body. It blows in waves. Outside, the moon shines, fat and yellow. Its light is dissolved by the white glare of the theatre tube lights.

Sathi stares at the moon. His heart beats loud and warm with longing. He does not know why, but it hurts. He wants to get up, but his stomach shrinks and pulls at his insides. Maybe he should make the effort. Go to the tea shop and drink a cup, eat a rusk.

He stands up and shoulders the soda-bottle holder.

—Soda! Colour soda . . . soda . . . colour!

He goes up and down the aisle once, his voice echoing loudly in the nearly empty theatre. No use, he thinks. Not one of these looks like the soda-drinking type. He walks to the ladies' section. One or two usually buy colour. But today no one really notices him. He walks back to the chair section and stops.

Karuvachi is coming up the stairs. She climbs slowly, holding a man's hand, leaning lightly on his shoulder. The man holds up the end of his dhoti in his left hand. His right hand is around Karuvachi's waist. He looks unsteady, clearly drunk. His fingers flash diamonds. A rich man.

Karuvachi has a jasmine garland in her hair. She looks like she has just got dressed a few minutes ago. Her brocade sari and powdered face glow. She wears her sari low on her slim waist. She looks thin and wispy, almost transparent. She concentrates on getting the man up the stairs.

She holds on to the chairs for support. He says something inaudible and pulls her to him. She allows herself be pulled into a sofa seat. She props him up and sits beside him. Karuvachi raises her hands above her head and stretches them, relieved and triumphant, as though she has managed to complete an arduous task. The man leans towards her, dropping his head on to her shoulder.

What is he trying to do? Sathi squints. He can see only her red sari and dark face, a huge butterfly.

Karuvachi comes to the theatre often, each time with a different man. Sometimes by herself. Sathi knows her well. He wants to go up to her and talk. What if the man objects? But he is clearly lost to the world. Sathi walks up to the sofa seats, clutching his iron holder tight. There are altogether fifteen sofa seats, arranged in a long row. The row is empty except for Karuvachi and the man.

She smiles when she sees Sathi, a smile that breaks the powder on her face into little cracks.

—Look at his chap, Sathi. Heavy as a corpse. Can't tell you how tired I am. Everything hurts. Give me a soda.

Her voice is like a child's, trusting and silky. She seems happy to see him.

—What, sister, new party? Look at those rings on his fingers, shining away!

—Rascal! So you've seen those already? Don't cast your evil eye on me, all right? If something goes wrong, I'll know why. No, he's not new. I know him from before.

Sathi pops open a soda bottle and hands it to her. He sits down in the sofa next to hers. The man's head hangs loosely forward. Strange sounds escape his throat.

—Soda. Sister, should I give him one too?

—You and your soda! The chap pestered me to go with him to the cinema and now look at him. Man's gone! Why wake him? He'll come around when the film ends.

Sathi stares at her, unable to take his eyes off her betel-nut stained lips. She hands him back the soda bottle and puts her hand into her blouse. She pulls out a small purse and takes out a five-rupee note.

—Sathi, go buy me an egg bonda and some betel leaves. Keep the change. No need to take that holder along. Leave it here.

Sathi feels that everybody in the theatre is looking at her. She seems unconcerned. She burps loudly and slides down into her seat. The sofa seats wear faded covers and their coir stuffing shows in places. Sathi leaves reluctantly, unable to part from her. He goes out, five-rupee note in hand.

He walks out into a glare of lights and hectic selling. The betel-nut man stands outside his shop, his eyes searching around. His wife sits inside, looking surly. The child cries, but she doesn't pay any attention to it. She continues to stare sullenly at her husband.

—Dai, Sathi, looks like your sister's here?

The tea-shop man smirks at the betel-nut man's wife from behind his counter. The two shops touch each other.

She turns her gaze away from her husband and glares at him.

Sathi understands why the betel-nut man is so excited and irritable. How can he go and buy betel leaves now? Sathi decides to go to the tea shop first.

—One egg bonda. For Karuvachi.

He keeps his voice low.

The tea-shop man packs two bondas in a newspaper and hands them over. He doesn't ask for money. Sathi doesn't offer him any. The betel-nut man is waiting for him, waiting to catch his eye.

Sathi moves into the tea shop. From here the betel-nut shop is not visible. And no one from there can see him either. The betel-nut man comes into the tea shop.

—What does she want?

His voice is barely audible.

—Betel leaves.

The betel-nut man leans over into his shop and picks up a few betel leaves.

—Here, come and take over. I'm going home!

It is his wife. The betel-nut man doesn't move, though his wife's voice is tight with anger.

—Shut up! If you open your mouth again . . .

He leans over and barks at her. He hands the betel leaves to Sathi.

—Come to the office room. This wretch is a nuisance.

Sathi nods and walks back to the theatre. The bell rings once, twice and stops. Time for the show. The lights go out as he enters. Sathi's feet stumble, surprised by the sudden darkness. He stops, pulls himself alert and tiptoes carefully to the sofa seats. The diamond-ringed man is fast asleep. His snores irritate the air, like a frog's rasping croak.

Once more, Sathi sits in the sofa next to Karuvachi. He stubs his feet on the soda-bottle holder.

—Careful!

She looks up at him. He bends down and pushes the holder under the seat next to him. He hands over the bondas and betel leaves to her.

His fingers graze her hands. They feel smooth and he wants to hold on to them. She appears unconcerned and eats her bonda.

—Sister, I have to go. The betel-nut man is waiting for me.

—Fellow's got an eagle's eye. Can't bear him, your betel-nut man. He's got hands like spades.

Sathi gets up, planting his feet firmly on the ground and walking towards the office room.

The betel-nut man must be in a real state, desperate and impatient. I'm in for it, thinks Sathi. And if I go the other way, I'll have to face the man's wife. Why does the bastard want to do this? He's married, he has a nice-looking wife. But one may have a wife like a parrot and still want a mistress who looks like a monkey.

He feels sapped and flops back into his seat

The betel-nut man paces up and down the corridor in front of the office room. He is bare-chested, his lungi hitched above his knees. His huge stomach bobs up and down as he walks. Sathi swallows back his distaste.

—Is that man with her awake? Or is he done for?

—Half and half. Asleep and awake.

The betel-nut man drags Sathi to him, puts his hand around his shoulders and speaks into his ears.

—Tell Karuvachi to come to the ladies' counter. Booking will be closed in ten minutes. Then the queue passage will be shut. We can go into the passage. She can go back soon. Go on, tell her. If she acts strange, come back and tell me. I'll handle her.

— . . .

Sathi shakes his head. He feels ill in his stomach. The betel-nut man sticks a two-rupee note into Sathi's pocket.

—Go and drink tea or something. But do this first.

He runs his hands through Sathi's hair and then walks towards the ladies' counter.

—Dai, Sathi! Sathi drags his feet back. —My wife's at the shop. If you open your mouth about this, I'll pull your intestines out! Careful.

—Me? Why would I say anything?

Sathi replies without looking at him and goes back in. The credits are showing. Karuvachi hands him a bonda. His hand goes out, lean and hungry, and grabs her outstretched palm. His heart quickens. His fingers shake as he takes the bonda.

—The betel-nut man wants me?

—Mmm . . . near the ladies' counter.

She sighs so loudly that he can feel it in his ear, a swirl of air. He finishes his bonda and wipes his hands on his lungi. He sits still, crossing his legs tightly.

—Look at him snore. Bloody steam engine!

Even in the dark, Sathi can see her pulling a face. He smells the jasmine in her hair and moves closer to her. The thick, sickly-sweet smell of talcum powder.

Sathi shivers though he is not cold. He feels flung into a hot cauldron, feels the heat all over him. He has seen her so many times, talked to her so often. But this is the first time he has felt like this. This excitement, this shame.

He can't possibly sit here any more. But how can he just get up? He looks at her face. She is watching the screen intently.

The hero has just finished peeing and is zipping his fly up. He turns back to look at her, then turns to the screen again. He does this several times.

—Sister.

He sounds lame and breathless.

She does not reply. Didn't she hear? Was his voice that weak? He swallows a mouthful of spit.

—Si . . . s . . . ter!

She doesn't say anything. The seat on which she sits has no arm rest. His hand lies on the edge of her seat. His eyes are on her, fixed, intense. His hand moves towards her, with a life of its own.

He finds her sari and then her waist. She does not move. Sathi shudders and places his palm on her waist. Gently at first, then surely, firmly. Her waist feels different from the film-reel man's tight flesh. His fingers knead her skin slowly.

He strokes her gently. He does not want to look at her. He looks away and stares at the screen instead. He feels shy, ashamed. He continues to stroke her. His palm moves downwards towards her stomach and finds her belly button. Then, upwards. It is easy, for she sits back and lets his hand wander up.

She continues to watch the film. When his fingers reach the last knot of her blouse, she slaps his hand away, but holds on to it. He can't stop now. He is afraid she will push him away. He holds her hand tightly.

—Sister!

His voice trails off, his eyes close in a haze of dream and want. He wants to bend down and kiss her there. He turns to her.

She looks at him and seeing him hopeless with longing, holds his face up by the chin. She bends and plants a deep, soft kiss on his lips.

He feels sapped, drained, and flops back into his seat. She pushes his hand away.

—Not even four hairs on your face and you want this! And you call me 'sister'.

—Sister, please, can't I go with you?

She pinches his cheek hard, arranges her sari neatly over her breasts and gets up. She walks towards the ladies' counter.

Sathi sits still. He closes his eyes tight. He wets his tongue. So close. He uncrosses his legs, lets his hands hang limply at his side, slack and hollow on his chair.

The diamond-ringed man is into his second round of snoring. Snores like groans. His head lolls on his chest. Should he have stopped Karuvachi from going? The man's breath is like a snake's hiss.

Sathi stands up and almost falls down. He stays still for a while and then ties his lungi tightly around his waist. He bends down and feels his own legs. Hairy. Should he have lifted his lungi and shown her? He runs a hand above his lips. Just fuzz. Maybe it will grow if he shaves often enough.

Sathi moves close to the sleeping man and pushes his fingers deep into his shirt pocket. His heavy lolling head presses against Sathi's groping hand. He pushes the head away and it drops off on the other side. The man continues to snore. Sathi pulls out a few coins and a half-smoked cigarette. He shoves the lot into his own pocket.

He feels inside the man's shirt and finds another pocket. His fingers brush against the moist, sticky hair on the man's chest. The man's face twitches, but he does not wake up. Nothing in the inside pocket. Sathi lifts up his dhoti and searches for his underwear pocket. He brushes against his thigh and draws back, disgusted.

—Dog!

He kicks at the man's leg and walks away.

He is almost at the exit when he remembers his soda-bottle holder. He comes back for it and walks out. He keeps away from the betel-nut shop. He goes to the soda shop, puts his holder away and walks towards the stairway. The Hulk comes up to him from near the office room, his face lit with sly glee.

—Dai, Sathi, come here!

The Hulk sounds playful and excited. Sathi looks up. The tea-shop man makes a sign at them, mimicking a slap, and winking in the direction of the betel-nut shop. Sathi does not want to go, but he follows The Hulk. He sees Mani and Ganesan in front of the booking counter on the ladies' side. They catch his eye, hold their hands to their mouths and giggle silently.

The counter is shut, the passage is in darkness. Its wall is panelled a few feet from the ground. Ganesan jumps up, manages to hold on to one of the lower slats and peers into the darkness. Mani tries to clamber up too, but fails. With a single jump, The Hulk is up on the wall and his hands find a hold. Sathi is too tired to jump and look. His body feels wrung-out like a rag.

—Mmm...

The Hulk slurps. Mani laughs loudly. The Hulk slurps again. Sathi calls out in a whisper:

—Dai, can you see anything?

Suddenly the betel-nut man is on them. He does not see Sathi, but his hand reaches out and hits Ganesan on his back. Ganesan screams and falls down. The Hulk tries to run away but gets hit too.

—Fuck your mothers! Rowdy dogs!

The betel-nut man slams his big hand against their bodies over and over. They cower and sprint away, yelling.

Sathi stands quietly in the darkness. The betel-nut man enters the queue passage and disappears. Sathi stares at the outside wall of the passage. Suddenly he jumps up and hangs on to a slat. He sees nothing. Only deep darkness. He puts his ear to the slats. Quiet. He does not climb down.

He stays there, hoping.

12

Laughter echoes around the huge empty room

Sathi wakes up. He feels something cool on his feet and on his nose. Now it is all over him. A coolness that does not make him shiver. It grabs his fingers and then, unexpectedly, lets go. The moment passes and he lies lifeless once more.

He lifts his head off the ground and tries to look around him. He cannot open his eyes—they are glued together. He waits for the coolness again and when it fails to come, thinks of that original moment with longing.

His body drips sweat and smells terrible. The dirt on his shirt sticks to his back and chest. He shifts his arms and legs. The sun pricks at his eyes. He holds up his forearm to keep the light from hurting.

Something cool and misty presses against his feet. Like water dripping slowly and rhythmically from a leaf.

He wants to hold on to the moment, lose himself in it. He does not move his hands. He cannot. His longing has a life of its own. It breaks into happiness. Subsides, starts again.

He yearns for something. He does not feel the cruel sun or the rough, uneven floor. Though tired from walking all night, his feet don't trouble him like they usually do. Even his scarred shoulders, worn out from carrying heavy soda-bottle holders, seem to have healed. His eyes, always heavy and ready for sleep, are alert. His ears, so used to taunts and abuses, open up to the world, fresh.

He prises his hot eyelids open and then he sees it. Only its smile is visible at first. The betel-nut man's child. The child laughs as Sathi opens his eyes slowly. He is now fully awake and the child loves this fact. It babbles and punches his nose. The blows lightly fleck Sathi's face.

He laughs at the child and it playfully hits him on his mouth. The child is dark and happy. It stands there, biting at the black thong around its neck. It holds its hands out to him. He must wake up and do its bidding.

Without getting up, Sathi draws the child to him. He places it on his chest. The child tries to free itself. Sathi kisses its cheek. The child screams and yells. It crinkles its dimpled face. Sathi lets go and the child bounces off him, but does not go away. It sits next to him and laughs again. Sathi is startled at this quick change—its crumpled face is happy again. He puts his hands out. The child slaps them away. It babbles and taps its fingers against his shirt pocket.

His cigarette pack sticks out of his pocket. Sathi gives it to the child. The child grabs the pack and tries to pry it open. The pack falls on Sathi's stomach and then on to the ground. The child squats and tries to get at the pack with both its hands. It drops the pack down and picks it up again. Its world shrinks into the pack. The child does not look at Sathi any more.

His fingers sneak up and he tickles it. The child roars with laughter. It laughs so much that saliva dribbles down from its mouth. Sathi lifts the child on to his stomach. He tucks its legs under, to sit comfortably.

—Thuri! Thuri!

Sathi makes up his own babble.

The child does not understand, but laughs. Sathi puts his hands over his eyes. The child tugs at them, trying to prise them away from his face. Sathi pulls his hands away suddenly. The child is delighted.

—Hello, little calf!

He draws his breath in, holds his stomach with both hands, puffs it out and says:

—Buuk!

The child loves it. It tries to push his hands away from his stomach. It spies a cigarette hanging loose from his pocket and takes it.

—Give that back to me, baby.

Sathi puts a hand out. It holds the cigarette tight and crushes it. The cigarette paper comes off and spills tobacco on him. Sathi laughs and so does the child. The child looks at its fingers and then at his stomach. A sprinkling of tobacco dust lies on Sathi's stomach, like a mess of worms. The child tries to gather the dust. It slips through the small fingers, again and again. The child is soon wrapped in its own game and Sathi is forgotten. The dust is all.

Sathi watches the child intently. He doesn't want to disturb the game. Finally, it gathers a small fistful of dust and, looking a little shamefaced, hands it over to him.

Sathi is up now, holding his hands out. The child runs away from him and into the heat, its black body shining.

—Aiy! Come back in, small thing.

The child runs faster, towards the water tank and the toilets. Sathi runs ahead and blocks its way. It looks around and runs towards the theatre verandah. It stops when it reaches there. There is a high step. The child tries to raise its leg and climb it. It leans back against the verandah edge and, with its hands firmly planted on the floor for support, tilts backwards and sits on the step. It turns and looks at Sathi triumphantly.

—Catch, catch, come and catch the baby!

Sathi pretends to jump on to the verandah and catch the child. The child giggles and begins to run again. It runs to the theatre doors and, with great effort, climbs the few steps that lead in. Sathi walks slowly behind it.

The theatre is empty except for a few sparrows that flutter and fly across the ceiling. The chairs and benches are relaxed, sleepy.

The child stops behind a chair. Sathi looks around, pretending not to have seen it. The child loves this game.

—Ah, there you are!

Sathi rolls his eyes and with his head down, moves with mock menace towards the child. Its laughter echoes around the huge empty room, bouncing off the walls and scattering in all directions. Sathi hitches his lungi above his knees and runs, holding it with one hand.

The child runs ahead without looking and almost bumps into the spit bucket. But Sathi is already there, catching it before it hits the bucket. He carries it like a baby rat. Bounces it, makes it laugh. This is all he wants to do.

He throws the child up and catches it as it comes down. It is afraid at first. But when it lands safely in his arms, it smiles. He throws it up in the air again.

Higher, higher and each time the child comes back snug into his arms, it gurgles louder. Laughs until it subsides into a helpless happy whimper. Sathi laughs too, lost in the joy of the moment. His eyes are wet with tears from laughing. His stomach contracts with happiness and hurts. The child is in no mood to stop. It drums at his hands and face, asking him to throw it up in the air again.

—Aiy! Motherfucker! Leftovers-eating dog!

Sathi looks up, shocked.

The child is grabbed from him. His face shrinks, all happiness suddenly drained from it. The child tries to jump out of the other pair of arms. Hands reach towards Sathi and it cries loudly. The betel-nut man's moustache quivers with anger.

—Rowdy dog! What do you think this is, a child or a wooden doll?

Sathi feels a hard slap burn across his face. His head reels and for a moment he cannot feel anything. When he comes back to himself, the man is gone.

The man walks through the door, the child on his shoulders. The child tries to free itself, its hands held out towards Sathi. It beats at its father's shoulders, wriggles and suffers in his arms.

Sathi sits down, feeling empty and slack inside.

13

A termite escaping a sudden patch of light

Night show. A crowd forms near the stairway, after the interval bell has rung.

The betel-nut man lives close to the theatre. He leaves as soon as he shuts down his shop late in the evening. The tea-shop man is from Monghur, but he has a cycle which he rides home after the interval. He only returns in the afternoon the next day. The soda man prefers to sleep at the theatre. He usually asks for his ramshackle cot to be brought out after the interval. He positions it near the stairs.

The soda man sits on his cot while the theatre boys mill around him. They bring him gossip, odd stories. Chatting away, he waits for sleep to take possession of him. He usually stays awake until Natesan finishes with the cycles.

He fancies himself the boys' friend and guide. Many of them do ask his advice on worldly matters. Sathivel prefers to just listen, content to smoke his ganja-filled cigarette. He lies on his back, staring up, blowing smoke into the air.

Natesan is usually high on his 'pill' at this hour. Sathi prefers ganja. It makes him dreamy, fills his empty stomach with haze and sends him to sleep. Most days, he manages one meal.

Except when a new movie is released. Then, for at least a day or two, business is good and he eats thrice a day. But once the good days pass, it's back to pleading with the soda man. He begs and harangues him for money. When new movies come along, his world brightens up. But not for long. He is soon back to wheedling. And so it goes.

Sathi thinks of his father and of The Hulk. The Hulk teases him about the old man, mimics his walk, folding his fingers into his palm, pretending they have been chewed up by leprosy. Sathi feels whipped then and wishes he could have an extra ounce of ganja.

A few puffs and his body feels light and easy, his mind free. He knows this won't last. The good feeling ebbs away gradually. And he always wants it back, that burst of pleasure that frees his mind. Immediately. It would help if he could take a smoke or two every hour.

Ganja consoles him, makes the hard, dirty earth a soft bed of cotton.

Maybe he should give in to the soda man's pressure, help him out at the farm, maybe graze those sheep. A trap, but food at least. He thinks this way once in a while, especially on the days that the film-reel man comes for him.

The film-reel man is persistent, stubborn. He's always there, without fail. He comes and stands by the stairway as soon as the interval is over. If Sathi happens to be late, or hides in a dark corner, the man goes crazy. He circles the theatre, looking for him. Worse, he sits in his room and howls.

Sometimes, when he has succeeded in getting Sathi into his room, he holds on to his feet and cries, whimpering like a hurt dog. Sathi feels it's all a game, a big elaborate show put up for his benefit. But he finds it difficult to ignore the man's tears. They have a hold on him, those tears, they stick to him like stubborn leeches. Besides, the man is good to him. He gives him cigarettes, sometimes even money.

The soda man's voice disperses his thoughts.

—Dai, Mani! So how does that tea-shop guy treat you? Well? Giving you enough money?

The soda man is seated in the middle of the cot. Half his body is sunk into it, while the other half sprawls out. Mani sits by his feet.

—Where, sir? Today, we sold for nineteen rupees. But he tells me he spent twenty-two. He cuts my pay. What can I do?

The soda man's head, sitting oddly on a body that is sunk into a mesh of rope and wire, shakes in disapproval. He lights a bidi and counsels Mani in a low voice.

—Chap's a bloody miser. No way to treat a boy who works. Look at me! Ask the lads how much I loan them. That Hulk—God knows how much I've given him. What can I do? You're mine, all of you. Today you borrow, tomorrow when you earn a bit more . . . on a good-movie day, I take my dues from you. Look at this son-of-a-bitch Sathi! When he came here, he was a fool. Knew nothing. Today, he's a man of the world. Man can't do without his ganja—what fine habits!

Sathi stubs the end of his burnt-out cigarette on the wall behind his head. He replies casually.

—You give me the money you owe me, master. Not more, not less. When I want more . . .

—More! You always ask for more! We'll talk the next time you come begging. When you come with your asshole burning and dry with hunger . . .

—I always pay you back. Always, when there's a good movie.

—What good movie? Where do we get good movies here? That bastard never brings any. When that Rainbow Theatre is ready, we'll be done for. Who'll come to this dirty place? Not one motherfucker.

The soda man clears his throat angrily and spits a dirty gob out.

—I won't do this forever. I'll shut down by the end of the year. Wait and see. What do I get, anyway, sitting here day and night, waiting for good movies?

—We get good ones sometimes.

Sathi is soothing.

—Like a fucking miracle! God knows where that old bastard gets his films. Once the fellow picked up four films for two thousand rupees. He knows nothing about cinema. But he thought he was smart—getting four films for the price of two. And then, when he started screening them, the first film didn't run past two days.

—Which one was that?

—That Mangamma movie. Ancient bloody thing. Ranjan does a double act in it. Then he showed *Haridas*, you know, with that singing hero, Thyagaraja Bhagavathar. Who the hell is interested? Not today's crowd. Then there was *Srivalli*. Not bad. Mahalingam plays Murugan, and Rukmini, today's Lakshmi's mother, is Valli. What a beauty she was! But what's the use? No one wants to see . . .

—I know that one. Full of songs!

—That's the one. The whole time. The last was, if I remember right . . . *Sabapathi*. With the comedian T.R. Ramachandran in it. Didn't make it through the day. Went flying out of the window. Ten people for the night show. Chaps from Aravur, escaping the mosquitoes in their town.

Paid a rupee and bought sleep. The movie went on and these chaps were out, snoring!

—Why did they bother—for ten people?

—You've got to screen it once you've announced it. And what about the honour of our theatre? Even that didn't last. The manager went crazy. Ran in and started throwing everyone out. Woke up those chaps and chased them out, just like that. Only one guy was awake and watching, all eyes. Had to be dragged out.

The soda man's eyes glint wickedly. He throws his head back and laughs loudly.

Sathi laughs too. He stands up, holds his stomach and roars. He sits down immediately and rests his swimming head against the wall, exhausted with the effort. He remains still for a moment, then laughs again. Then, again. He can't control himself now. He holds on to the sides of the cot and screeches. Mani begs him to stop, but ends up laughing himself.

—Sathi! Come! Right away!

Ganesan suddenly bursts in on the group.

—What for? Tell me first. Sathi slows down, wiping his tears.

—What, Ganesaa? A new bit of sari?

—Forget it, master. No such luck! There's a chap sleeping inside. His slippers have fallen off his feet. Looks like they are new.

A termite escaping a sudden patch of light

Sathivel sits up.

—Where?

—Bench seat. Third row from the floor tickets. In the corner.

—You talk a lot, Ganesaa. You boast that you'll whip your master one of these days and you can't even lift a pair of slippers!

—Master! Can't help it, master! Sathi's better at this sort of thing. He's used to it. Natesan's good too, but he's out there sleeping. Shall I wake him, Sathi?

—Come, show me.

Sathi gets to his feet and shuffles towards the theatre.

Ganesan goes in first, followed by Sathi. Mani goes after them, but slips into one of the chair seats. Sathi and Ganesan find their way to the benches. Not too many people tonight. The ladies' section is almost empty.

They see him—lying on his stomach on one of the empty benches. His head drawn in, he sleeps with his feet facing the door. There is still a bit of space left on the bench, near his feet. On the other side, by his head, sits another man.

Sathivel sits down quietly by the sleeping figure. Ganesan pretends he is searching for something and goes past Sathi up the aisle. After a while, he sneaks out through the exit.

On screen, someone sings a sad song. A man walks in a graveyard, his hands spread out against a long, wide evening sky, yowling.

Sathi looks under the bench.

The people are silent, captured by the lines of the sad song that pricks at them from the screen.

Sathi sees them. The slippers are lying on the floor, away from him, directly beneath the man's head. He wonders if anyone is watching him. He sits on the edge of the bench and extends his foot towards the slippers. His foot darts forward, like a termite escaping a sudden patch of light. But he still can't get at them. The man is tall and his head is far away from where Sathi sits. The man on the other side is lost in the film.

Sathi sits back and watches the screen for a whole minute. The sleeping man stirs. He turns and sleeps on his back. His lungi shifts, exposing a leg. Sathi wriggles his body, pretending to be irritated that the stranger's feet have touched him. He gets up and moves to the bench behind.

Now he is directly behind the man's head. The sad song is almost over. There are two more people on his bench, but they are at the far end. Sathi sits back. The sleeping man moves again. Sathi decides to wait until he is safely and fully asleep. On the screen, the singing man's face is full and tragic.

A termite escaping a sudden patch of light

'*O God who created mortal men . . .*'

The song sounds far away, as though the singer were sitting in a deep well. He hears a gentle snore, the even breath of a man in deep sleep. Sathi stretches both legs out as far as they can go. He holds his body still while his legs move under the bench.

His foot feels the hard edges of rubber and stops. Using his toes, he silently picks up the pair of slippers, one with each foot, and pulls them towards him. He draws his right foot in first and then waits. Resting his weight on it, he slowly pulls in the left. Smooth, careful.

He waits a moment and then gets up holding his crotch, like someone who has to piss urgently. He rushes out. The slippers are on his feet. No one seems to have noticed anything. He goes straight to the piss-puddle next to the water tank, crouches and pees. He gets up and walks slowly towards the stairway. Mani is waiting for him.

It is odd to walk with slippers. They feel like small rocky slabs. They are also far too big for him. The slippers flap as he walks. If he wore them for a day or two, he could get used to them. He wants to walk away from the stairway and find Natesan. They've got to hide the slippers somehow. Maybe tomorrow they can sell them for twenty rupees. Or maybe keep them.

Sathi's feet feel fluid. He turns and looks behind him. No one in sight. Long, narrow slits of light and shadow from the screen filter through the exit doors. Sathi's eyes are arrested for a minute by the flickering images.

He cannot get away, he knows. Mani and Ganesan are there by the stairway. They stand on either side of the cot, two stout demons guarding a temple gate.

—Let's see! Let's see!

Ganesan runs towards him, his arms waving. He looks like he's going to swoop down and grab the slippers from his feet. The soda man looks at Sathi's feet. He bounces out of the cot, rummages inside the shorts he wears under his lungi and brings out a small key. It is the key to the soda shop.

—Here! Give them to me!

He drags Sathi towards the shop. He opens the door and makes Sathi take the slippers off his feet. He flings them inside and locks the door. He turns towards the cot, then again towards the door. He opens the shop a second time and goes in. He picks up the slippers and hides them between two wooden crates. He does this in the dark, without switching the shop light on. He then walks back and lowers himself into the cot.

Sathi follows him and lies down on the ground. Mani and Ganesan sit on the far side of the cot and light bidis.

The soda man opens a fresh packet of bidis and gives one to Sathivel. He lights his own and passes the flame to Sathi. Quiet all round, except for the eloquent glow of bidis.

Ganesan stubs his bidi out on the ground and stands up. His voice drops into a low hiss.

—The fellow's woken up. He's coming...

Sathi lights a second bidi. Ganesan sits by the cot. They start a conversation.

—What, Ganesa! Do you at least get paid these days?

—Where do I get to see money? On good days, I ask for my share. But the bastard lies and messes with the accounts. When I ask for cash, he says I still owe him. I'll get him one of these days, you'll see.

Ganesan looks behind him as he replies.

The man is indeed coming towards them. He has gathered his lungi over his knees. His face is dark with sleep. His hair is a tangled mess. It stands up, like a small tower. The man is with them now. He glances at the boys but addresses the soda man.

—Slept off in there. My slippers were on the floor. Some bastard swiped them. Brand new slippers, they were. Son of a bitch!

He looks like he's ready to haul the thief off and give him a hiding.

—Where?

Sathi sounds concerned.

—Bench ticket. I was lying down. Couldn't have slept for more than five minutes. When I woke up, they were gone. Brand new, I bought them last week.

—Tch! Tch! Sathi sympathizes. —Didn't see anyone after the interval. We've been sitting here all the time. Thief must be still inside!

—Motherfucker!

The man curses on, words tumbling from his mouth. They echo strangely in the dark. The man puts his hand into his lungi and pulls out a small torchlight from the pocket of his shorts. He flicks it on. It lights up a tiny patch of the night.

He walks towards the theatre, comforted by the up-and-down bobbing of the light. Halfway up, he turns around and walks back. He addresses the soda man.

—You'll be here, sir?

—Hmm? I'll be here.

He walks away. The soda man turns to Sathi.

—Smart man. He's no fool, see? But you—you're smarter. Bloody devil. You're even better than that long-legged Singaan.

—Him! Why bring his name up? Fellow's not worth my moustache.

Sathi grinds his teeth and spits the words out in angry disarray. He breathes excitedly.

—Dai, dai! What's all this now? Quarrelled with Singaan?

—I'm going to break his bones one day. When the bastard swipes something, he keeps it all to himself. But when I get hold of something, he wants a share. Dog!

—All right, all right. Don't yell. That slipper guy may come out again. Quiet. And sleep.

Ganesan walks up to the office room. He slides towards the theatre doors, peeps in and returns.

—I looked inside, master. The chap's looking everywhere. He's flashing his torch at everyone's feet!

—Well, well! Told you he's a smart fellow! Must be a miserly weaver. Only they'd go so far!

Sathi looks up.

—Wish I'd known about his torch. Could have got that too. Had it in his shorts, though.

The night settles into a calm. But not for long. Sathi hears voices raised in anger. He opens his eyes and looks in their direction. The slipper owner is out, standing by one of the exit doors. The door is slightly open. There is another man with him. They seem to be arguing. One raises his hand and the other shrugs.

Sathi looks beyond them. His eyes fix momentarily on the screen. A woman is crying. She is beautiful in a strong-featured way. She sobs on and on, till her face grows puffy with tears.

Sathi turns to the soda man.

—Looks like he's caught hold of someone.

—Shit!

Everyone is up and looking. The men argue. Their voices reach the stairway group as a faint ring of words.

A few others come out of the theatre, roused by the sound of voices. They stand for a while, then go back in.

What does it matter to them? Though this is something, they would rather die than miss a song.

Suddenly, the slipper owner grabs the other man's hand and drags him towards the soda man's cot. His voice reaches the cot before he does.

—Brother! Look, this son-of-a-whore has got my slippers. He's even wearing them. Caught him, see? But he's refusing to give them back. Says they're his, that he bought them!

It is the other man's turn now.

—Dai! I'll tear every nerve from your body! Be careful. The soda man is my friend. He knows me! Brother, you know Pundur Chandran, don't you? I'm his brother. You've seen me around? This chap must have gone after a whore and left his slippers there. And he bothers me for them.

The slipper owner cuts in before the soda man can answer. He looks like he is about to knock the other man out.

—Who's bothering whom? Bother yourself! These slippers are mine! I know them like my mother knows me.

—Brother! Tell him. You know me. I bought these yesterday, from that shop near the statue. Hold on, I may even have the bill.

He fishes in his pockets and comes up with a much-crumpled bill, folded several times over. The soda man finally gets his chance to mediate. He peers at the paper.

—So that's settled. The fellow's not lying. See, he's got a bill. And I know the family. Honest sort of people. Go look for your slippers somewhere else.

The slipper owner edges away, muttering to himself as he walks out. The other man continues to whine.

—The chap didn't know who I was. Let him come to Pundur. I only have to raise a finger and he's done for. The lads there will beat him to a pulp.

—Leave it. He has his sorrow—new slippers, after all. Go and enjoy the rest of the film.

The soda man makes it clear he does not wish to pursue the subject.

—Damn!

His voice is triumphant and tired. He sinks into his cot and stretches out. Sathi is already asleep, relieved that he can sail away at last.

—Sathi! Aiy! Sathi! The soda man calls to him. —Those slippers. Leave them inside the shop! I'll take them home tomorrow. You can have five rupees for them. Okay?

Sathi drifts out of sleep. He wants to reply, but his mouth does not open. He tries to move his lips, coax words out of them. He fails and the words die in his throat.

14

Wet sand sits well in ploughed-up areas

It is well past interval time. The second half of the night show is on, but no one is sleeping. The usual crowd is gathered by the stairway. The soda man does not trust them to stay. He knows they will disappear into the shadows if he so much as takes his eyes off them. Which is why he has sent Sathi alone to town to buy the whole group a meal of prottas and chutney. He waits anxiously for Sathi to return. His eyes wander to the gate from time to time.

—That dog Sathi! Where's he gone? Think he found some ganja and passed out on the road somewhere. As always, The Hulk is impatient.

—Dai! Shut up, will you? He has to wait till that fellow makes forty prottas. Think it'll be done in a minute? And maybe they don't have enough chutney.

The soda man's tone is conciliatory, though he is impatient as well. He is in his green shirt—the one with the big collar that he wears only for coming into the theatre and going home. It is a big shirt, reaching almost to his knees. Near his cot by the stairs stand five cycles with carriers attached to them. They have been hired for the night.

—Only prottas, master? Nothing to drink?

—Don't worry! I'm sure he's arranged for something. Who'll agree to this job, otherwise?

The young men bait the soda man.

—There's Sathi!

The Hulk sees him coming in. Sathi pushes his cycle with one hand. The other holds his lungi to his thin waist. His shirt buttons are all open and his chest is heaving and sweaty. A heavy bag hangs from one of the cycle's handlebars. His eyes look lost.

The Hulk runs up and grabs a parcel from the bag. Sathi loses his balance. He lets go of the cycle, which falls down.

—Dai, Hulk! Slowly—can't you wait?

The soda man scolds The Hulk gently. Any other time, he would have slapped him. But not tonight.

Sathi tightens his lungi around his waist, picks up his cycle and places it against a wall. The bag is passed around and everyone has his own parcel of food. Sathi joins them.

He opens his own and then stops. He looks around. Natesan is not there. He picks up another parcel, repacks his own and walks towards the cycle stand.

—Heh, heh! Going in search of your wife?

The Hulk cackles. Sathi turns and glares at him. Mani looks at Sathi and then at The Hulk.

—Natesan is his wife? The other day you said Sathi was the film-reel man's wife. What is this Sathi? A man or a woman?

—Neither this nor that. What else?

Sathi does not hear them. He is far away now, near the cycle stand. Outside, all is quiet. Except for the lights on the main road, there is not a soul around. Sathi is suddenly afraid of the huge night, the silence. His head down, he hurries to the cycle stand. Not too many cycles—only a single row standing against the wall.

Natesan has laid his lungi across the row of cycle carriers and is fast asleep. His thin face looks peaceful.

Sathi puts the food packets down in a corner. He runs his hand over Natesan's face, then pinches his cheek gently. Natesan makes a hissing sound, shifts, and continues to sleep, his head pressed against a cycle seat. Sathi slaps his stomach, pulls at his limbs.

—Natesaa!

He gets up, but barely.

—What?

His voice is choked with fatigue. Sathi opens a packet and hands it to him. He takes the other and climbs on to a cycle carrier himself. The packet has three dry, wrinkled prottas and a fiery looking sauce.

—The bastard expects us to eat this shit and do his dirty work for him?

Natesan tears a piece of protta.

—And he grumbled even for this. But the other guys—they don't care. The soda man's been promising everyone toddy when we get there. They're drooling already.

—We should never have agreed to this. Should have asked for money. Fifty rupees each.

—Him and money! You think he'd cough up? Rather strip us dead than give us money!

—Well, he's got to strip himself of cash if he wants such things done!

Natesan growls. A hiccup cuts him short.

Sathi taps him on the head with his knuckles.

—Slowly, slowly. What's the hurry?

They finish eating and wipe their hands on their lungis. They want water. They walk back into the theatre compound towards the water tank. Just then the bell rings. End of show. May as well wait and get the cycles out. Natesan unlocks the chain to which all the cycles are hooked. Sathi pulls out each cycle and passes it to the owners.

The theatre doors continue to throw the crowd into the roads. Sathi and Natesan push their way through the mass of heads leaving. They go to the soda shop first. Sathi unlocks the door, throws the cycle chain in and picks up the soda man's bag. He locks the door behind him. They walk towards the water tank.

By the time they reach the stairway, everyone is ready. The old watchman is almost done locking the theatre doors. Five cycles stand next to each other. The Hulk takes the first, Periasamy the second, Ganesan the third, Vattan the fourth and Sathi the fifth. Each of them has to take someone on his carrier. The soda man of course has his own cycle. He is to take Sanmugan with him. They look impressive, as if they are part of a cycle race. Twelve people in all.

—Master, if you'd told me about the job earlier, I'd have brought Singaan along. He's the man for you. He'd tear that fellow's face apart. The Hulk boasts, as usual.

—No one's seen Singaan around. Only turns up when there's a new film. Where do you think you're going to find him? Sathi wheels his cycle out of the gate.

The Hulk meanwhile has picked up a fight with Mani, refusing to take him on his cycle. The soda man intervenes and settles the matter. Natesan runs to the soda shop, drops his packet of cycle passes in and hops on to Sathi's cycle.

—Aiy! Is everyone going? I'll be all alone! And it's a dark night!

The old watchman whines.

They speed away and are soon eaten up by the dark. Their voices die in the black air. The road is a good one for the most part and they cycle along fast. Past the market area and the petrol pump, the road slopes upwards. There are a few people around. Oil lamps light the insides of tiny shops. They stop and buy bidis and cigarettes.

Sanmugan jumps off the soda man's cycle and comes running to Periasamy.

—Brother! I'll sit in the front! Don't want to be with the old man!

—Let's have tea!

Sathi calls out.

He darts a quick glance at the soda man. His face is in shadow, and Sathi can't make out how the man reacts to his request.

—Why now? He barks out.

—Sathi, forget it. Let's go on. The chap says he'll give us toddy. Why bother him for a silly cup of tea? You're such a dumb dog!

The Hulk hisses into Sathi's ears. Sathi nods in agreement, but calls out.

—Master, at least some chips.

The soda man goes into one of the shops and buys a packet of chips. When he comes back, they pedal away.

Sanmugan, now perched in front of Periasamy's seat, is cheerful. The soda man brings up the rear, alone.

—Dai! Hulk! If someone beats me, I'll probably die. But not you. You're the only one who can take a beating. Come, cycle in front!

Sanmugan taunts The Hulk.

—Want me to take it all? What about your pretty asses? Don't you all eat? Why the fuck should I go in front?

—We'll run away! What do we care? It's you and your soda man. Your fate, not ours!

They continue to tease The Hulk. They love to see him angry.

—Yes, I'll get beaten up and you—you'll wipe your asses and run!

The soda man wants them tonight to help settle a personal score. He and his cousin have quarrelled over a single-file path that leads to the soda man's house. The path goes through the other man's fields. True to its name, only one person can walk through it at a time, and even then, slowly, to avoid falling into the fields.

There was no question of driving a bullock-cart down that path. It had to be widened by ten feet before that could happen. The soda man wanted it done, but the cousin would not hear of it though the fields—and the path—were common family property.

The village elders tried to reason things out with him, but he was stubborn.

—Did he ask me when he built his house there? If that soda-seller wants a road, let him fight for it. Let him file a case in court against me.

One day, when the soda man was complaining to his friends at the theatre, the tea-shop man had made a suggestion.

—Forget about talking to your cousin. Nothing will come of talk. Take these theatre lads with you. Choose a moonless night. Quietly widen the road. Let's see what happens after that!

—Not a bad idea! But why these boys? Why don't I go to the market and find some down-and-outs there? Buy them some food and toddy and they'll do anything. Call one, and the others come running.

—Those market types! Just go to the taxi stand and ask for them. Tell them about your cousin. They'll cut him into pieces and feed him to the dogs! But they'll want plenty of money and more toddy. And you've got to be careful that they don't turn on you if they don't get enough!

—Oh . . . then I'll take my boys. Mine and the ones who work for that bastard manager. Those dogs can take on two chaps, can't they? I can get a few fellows from the village to dig the road. The boys can guard them in case there's any funny stuff.

So the soda man had made up his mind. The boys would listen to him, do what he told them to. He only had to arrange it—choose a good night, a new moon night. Take them to his house after the night show. Finish up things, let them off at dawn.

They are on Pasavur Road. The road is ill lit, with almost no street lights. They cycle through it and into Acchoor. It is a dirt road now, wet and squishy with the recent rain.

Ganesan tries to speed ahead and falls. He and his passenger get up. He picks up his bike and pedals fast to catch up with the others. His clothes are stained with sludge but he does not mind.

The soda man cycles slowly, hunched over his bike. He can't be hurried up. The boys joke that they can make it to Sadaiyur, a few hundred miles away, by the time he arrives.

Now the road is flanked by mud canals for carrying the run-off water from the catchment tank. But that happens only when it rains heavily. At other times, the canals are empty ditches. The cyclists veer off the road into the ditches and ride happily and defiantly through them. Alarmed frogs croak after them as they speed away, jubilant and excited.

They are finally on the single-file path. It runs through fields grown thick with peanut plants. The bicycles wobble, finding it hard to keep to the path in the dark. They reach the soda man's house. Someone switches on a light as the cycles ride up.

It is a tiled house, with a well-made path leading to it. Near it, but at a respectable distance, stand two barns. The door to the main house opens a little and the soda man's wife peeps out. She recognizes Natesan.

—Oh, it's you. Where is he?

—Coming slowly, sister.

—All right, go in there and wait.

She points to one of the barns and then shuts the door.

They enter the larger of the barns. The floor is wet with rain. The corner is stacked with firewood and dried corn stalks. In the middle of the hut is a buffalo calf, tied to a peg. The young men take their cycles into the barn and line them against the wall. They sit on the carriers. The soda man cycles in slowly. At last.

—Aiy! I mean you!

He gets down from his bike and whispers loudly.

His wife opens the door and looks out. He barks at her in a low, savage voice.

—Why the hell did you switch the light on? Want to show us up? Whose side are you on?

Wet sand sits well in ploughed-up areas

She slips inside quickly and puts out the light. A dog trots in from somewhere, barking loudly. The soda man asks his wife for a lantern and goes out to quieten the dog. When he manages to stop it from barking, he comes to the barn and calls Sathi and Natesan out. They follow him into his house.

A well-made, wide outer room, nicely cemented. Sathi longs to roll on the smooth floor. It was probably used as a storage space once. Past the outer room lies a covered courtyard. Beyond the courtyard are two living spaces.

The soda man picks up a heap of jute sacking from the courtyard and hands it over to the boys.

—Take these. You can sit on them.

Sathi and Natesan walk out, their hands heavy with jute, taking the soda man's lantern with them. They hear people arguing as they leave the house. They walk back to the barn and lay the sacking out carefully. Everyone sits back comfortably on the warm jute.

In a while, the soda man enters the barn. There is another person with him. They carry with them two big bottles of toddy, the packet of chips that was bought earlier in the evening and two tin cups.

—Shh . . .

The soda man holds a finger to his lips and puts everything on the floor. The boys lower their voices.

The two men leave the room immediately.

As soon as they are gone, Natesan grabs one of the cups and fills it with toddy. He shuts his eyes tight, leans back and drinks it up in one huge gulp. Some drips down his mouth as he puts the cup down. He clears his throat, spits, then picks up a handful of chips and stuffs them into his mouth. Sathi picks up his cup, while The Hulk takes the other. They empty their cups like Natesan. The others can barely wait for their turn.

The soda man hears them scuffling and comes in to warn them.

—Shh . . . quiet!

The toddy is freshly drawn, delicious.

—Mmm . . . what a beauty!

Sathi wipes his lips.

The barn is quiet, except for pleased murmurs and the clearing of throats.

After knocking back two full cups, Mani slips into a stupor. He stays still for a while, then starts rolling slowly across the barn. Even before they are done with the two bottles, the soda man brings in two more.

—Dai, dai! Careful! Don't drink too much. Keep steady. We've got a job to do.

He looks sober, stable. No smell of toddy on him.

By the third bottle, Mani starts to vomit.

—Who brought this fellow along? Can't even eat spicy food without throwing up!

No one replies. Or bothers to. Mani falls asleep, tired, face patched with vomit.

Sathi is happy.

For once, he doesn't crave ganja. But he still feels that the high from ganja is different, a warm, rich haze. Toddy fills him up, but he cannot sink into it. He wants to be up, throw something at someone, break a bottle.

Natesan crawls closer to Sathi.

—Sathi, Sathi, my dear.

He hugs him and kisses him on both cheeks. He holds him so tight that Sathi can hardly move.

—Sathi! What will I do without you? Where'll I go?

He falls into Sathi's lap and cries. He insists on lying there, burying his head in the thin folds of Sathi's lungi.

—Dai, Natesaa, dai! What's all this? Get up! Sathi is worried. He shakes Natesan, pulling at his hair.

Just then, the soda man comes in with a group of men.

—Come, come. Time to get to work!

Everyone rises to his feet, except Mani. Some of them can barely stand, but they try their best. The Hulk tips the last bottle to his mouth, grabs a handful of chips and scrambles after the soda man.

Everyone is armed—either with a scythe or a crowbar. It is not dark outside any more. The yard in front of the house has been lit. The men who came into the barn with the soda man get to work, widening the single-file path. They have crowbars and huge baskets of sand with them. The boys stand guard in a wide circle around them, weapons in hand.

The peanut plants smell fresh. They have thrown out fresh shoots a week ago and are now wide-leaved and thickly green.

The diggers slash at the crop, ploughing the ground around them until they have a few yards of rough road. Then they fill the dug-up area with sand. They have to carry on for another two hundred yards at least. As the diggers move forward, their guards move with them.

The soda man calls out to Sathi.

—Dai, Sathi! Look out, okay? If you hear the smallest sound, go for it! Just beat the shit out of them! That bastard cousin of mine should come and fall at my feet!

—Who the fuck will stand in my master's way? Come on, who's this?

—Ha! Who says I can't widen the road to my master's house! Let him bring his mother to me. I'll put her on the ground and . . .

It is The Hulk who shouts, unmindful that his lungi has slipped down from his waist and lies on the soggy ground.

—Keep a good eye out! That fellow is a bad one.

The soda man points to his cousin's land. They look around, but see no one. The soda man remains edgy. He keeps looking this way and that. The diggers work steadily and quietly. As they move down the path and away from the house, the light from the yard is no longer enough. Muthu, the soda man's son, comes running with a hurricane lamp.

—You! Who asked you to come here? Get back home. Now!

The soda man hisses at his son. The boy turns back, but stops short.

It is Sathi, beckoning to him. Even in the middle of all the stealth, he wants to get at Muthu. Muthu hesitates for a moment and then scurries back home.

The guards stand in a half-circle, blocking the working men off from prying eyes. Natesan has hitched up his lungi till it is only a fold of cloth around his hips. He stands, twirling a stick in his hand and walking around in circles.

—Aiy, Sathi! Look at me! MGR! Come, let's see you fight me!

—Me? Fight you? Want to be buried here?

—Come on!

—All right, you come on.

Sathi and Natesan draw close to each other, holding their weapons high. The soda man rushes between them and pulls them apart.

—A bit of toddy and see how you behave. Can't hold still? Showing off, stupid bastards! I ask you to keep guard and you play games!

Sathi and Natesan move away to opposite sides of the path and stand in the middle of the peanut crop. Behind them, the path is now a wide road. But there is still a long way to go.

The diggers continue to fill the sides quickly. The wet sand sits well in the ploughed-up areas. Now only two men dig, the others move back and forth filling mud and sand.

Bored with standing still, The Hulk joins the mud fillers.

—Fucking Hulk! Get out of there and go stand in front. I want you there. That fellow, my cousin, he's a big, nasty bastard. Careful—he's waiting to do something, I know it.

But the countryside is silent. The cousin's house, visible in the distance, is quiet. The Hulk gets back to his post.

One of the diggers jumps up. A huge bandicoot scuttles past the group into the fields. The guards run after it, but stop, as it moves too far away. Only Natesan follows it, stick in hand.

—Natesaa! Don't go anywhere. Come back!

The soda man shouts after him.

Natesan straggles back, emerging from the dark into the dull glow of the lamp. His legs are covered with soggy red soil. He is short of breath. One of the diggers looks up.

—What, Uncle, your cousin's gone silent? Pissing in his lungi, is he? Got frightened seeing these puny lads?

The man's face drips with sweat. His throaty breath and the slight hiss of the hurricane lamp make an odd rasping sound.

—Hmm. I don't trust him. He's no fool. He's thinking of something . . .

The soda man is still not sure that all will be well.

As the night pushes on, the guards grow tired. And bored with doing nothing. They are also drunk. The Hulk sits down and lights a bidi. Natesan sits as well, his back to the field's edge. Sathi collapses on to the ground beside The Hulk. He borrows The Hulk's bidi, takes a couple of puffs and hands it back. The bidi is passed back and forth. Just as its glowing end threatens to drop off into a heap of ash, Natesan's hand reaches for it.

At that moment, a hard, solid blow lands on his back.

15

A dead, dry voice

Sathivel lies curled at the foot of the stairs that curves its way up to the cabin room. The sun's hot rays have swallowed half his body. Streams of sweat run down him. His lungi has fallen off, lying rumpled and forlorn next to him. He sleeps, oblivious to the world. This sleep is not entirely natural. He has not eaten for a while and he is partly in a daze of ganja. Now and then he opens his eyes and shifts, but has no desire to get up. He lies on his stomach, then on his back. His hair is matted, spread out, gone completely brown at the roots. There is more fuzz on his face now. A beard that is almost there. He hears voices, loud ones. Maybe it is part of a dream. A dream in which someone talks nonsense all the time.

Sathi lies there for a long, long time. Until someone slaps his face. A stinging slap. He turns over and slowly opens his eyes. The sun hurts him. He sits up, searches for his lungi. He pulls it towards him, manages to get it around his waist.

—Dai! Your master wants you. Come!

It is Vattan.

—Tell him I'll come later. Now push off.

—Sathi, dai, listen. You've been like this since Natesan went. Come, come along.

— . . .

—Get up! You look like you're possessed.

Sathi feels tiredness in every pore of his body. He slumps down and stretches himself. He wants to go to sleep. He has been up all night, sticking posters in town. Bits of glue, now congealed into scabs, remain stuck to his legs. He has only slept since five in the morning.

Sanmugan bends down and touches him gently on his cheek. He is excited about something.

—Sathi, someone broke into the soda shop at night and took all sorts of stuff! Come!

Sathi looks up. Is he lying just to get him up? He shakes his head. Sleep begins to drain off him slowly.

—Dai, come now. That soda man's shouting for you.

A small crowd has gathered outside the soda shop. The tea-shop owner is part of the group. In the middle of this knot of people stands the soda man, looking defeated.

—I locked it up myself. After the night-show interval. I've got a good lock. Look—every night I pull at it to make sure. But the bastards haven't touched the lock. They got in some other way. How? You tell me, how? How'll I ever know?

He sees Sathi coming towards the shop. His voice hardens and his eyes turn sharp and mean.

—Dai, Sathi! When did you come in? Did you come by the shop?

—No, master. I was out putting up posters. Got back early in the morning and went off to sleep. I just got up.

—That leftovers-eating dog Natesan is gone. Who else? Who else would dare do this? Has to be you, you bastard!

The soda man jumps at Sathi, grabs him by the hair and slaps him hard on both cheeks. The slaps hit the morning quiet, like several soda-bottle tops popping out together. Sathi is taken aback. He has not expected this. The soda man drags Sathi to the shop.

—Look! Look at it! Completely ruined . . .

He pushes Sathi into the shop.

Sathi looks around him. The crates lie broken. The change box is on the floor, empty. The water tank is full of coloured powder, an angry soup. Splinters of wood and glass lie everywhere.

The place looks like a minor battleground—like a scene in the movies, after a brisk fight sequence. There probably was not much in the change box. The soda man only leaves small change behind and takes the big notes home. But still! The rest of the shop has had it. Plenty of cleaning and repairs to do. And buying—new crates, bottle holders . . .

Sathi feels his mouth go dry. He tastes a big ball of something in his throat.

The soda man attacks him again.

—Say you did it! You! It must be you!

He punches Sathi in the face, in his stomach. Sathi's nose hurts. May be broken. He hears voices from the crowd calling to him.

—Say yes! Say you did it!

—Dirty leftovers-eating dog! Think you've done a great job, don't you? The soda man kicks him again and he falls on his face. His forehead hits one of the holders lying outside the shop. He wants to say something, but cannot. The crowd begins to disperse.

Sanmugan helps him stand and walks him to the verandah near the stairway. He sits down. Blood and saliva dribble down from his mouth. The soda man continues to hurl curses at him. Words swirl about in his mouth and are spewed out like spit.

Sathi wipes his face with the edge of his lungi and thinks. Who could it be? The Hulk? He doesn't seem to be around. But does The Hulk have a key? It must be someone with a key—the lock wasn't broken. The Hulk must have got tired of begging the soda man for money. Which is why . . .

Or maybe it wasn't The Hulk at all.

Sathi smiles to himself. His heart is humming. Someone has done what he dared not do. That's something.

It is almost one. The afternoon crowds will come in a while. Right now, there is no one at the gate, except for the usual hangers-on. The soda man must have come in early—a new film is being screened today.

The outer gate screeches. The old watchman. He walks in, contentedly, slowly, relishing his tobacco. He has probably been home for lunch. His shrunken body and bobbing head seem disconnected. As if they belong to two different people. He has a bunch of keys with him.

When he sees him, the soda man runs to the gate.

—Motherfucker! This old bastard must have done it. Look how he walks. So careless, so cocky! Dai, old goat!

The soda man falls on the old man and pummels him. He punches him on his face, his back.

The watchman just holds his face and cries.

—Oh my God! Oh! Oh!

He cowers, ducks, tries his best to fend off the blows. He falls down, rolls over. But the soda man is relentless. He kicks at the fallen old man. The keys drop from the watchman's hands. He crouches, then manages to stand up and begins to run.

The soda man catches up with him. He trips him up and pulls him by his flimsy inner shirt. The shirt tears and comes away in the soda man's hands. He lets go and the watchman falls down.

—Aiyo! Aiyo!

The watchman's eyes are dry. He is too afraid to cry. But he continues to scream.

—Dai, old jackal! There's no one around here but you. You have the keys to everything. You opened my shop, didn't you? Tell the truth! Bastard! How many times have I let you have soda free? Why did you do this to me?

The soda man gnashes his teeth and the words come out crunched. He kicks the old man again. The watchman raises his hands over his head and pleads with the soda man.

—Master, not me. It wasn't me!

No one dares to go near the old man. By now there is a large crowd at the gate.

—Aiy! Speak the truth! You did it!

—Aiyo! I don't know a thing . . .

The old man is crying now. He cannot speak. His words drown in a fit of anguished tears. He tries to get up but cannot. The soda man stands by furious, helpless.

—It's got to be him! He has the keys. Dirty old dog! He's finished me!

The crowd begins to move away.

The betel-nut man speaks up.

—Uncle! Why not tell the theatre owner? You never know.

—Oh yes, and what'll that old bastard do? Scratch my cock?

The watchman has managed to get up. He limps over to the stairway and sits down. His body shakes now and then and he continues to cry.

—Uncle, look at this.

The betel-nut man pulls triumphantly at the tin sheet that is jammed above the soda-shop door. The sheet has been nailed in there a long time ago, to hide the gap between the door and the roof. It looks bent now, like someone has tampered with it.

The betel-nut man holds it up and grins. The soda man's face darkens.

—Dai, Sathi! Where's The Hulk?

Sathi does not reply. He sits, his head down, staring at his feet. His lips are swollen and heavy.

—Sanmuga! Go and see. Check everywhere.

Sanmugan runs off. No one inside the queue passage, except Ganesan. Inside the theatre, only Periasamy, sleeping on the chairs. Near the booking room, the ladies' counter, by the cabin stairway.

No Hulk.

—So! It's The Hulk.

Sathi smirks to himself. The Hulk? How could The Hulk's fat body fit into that narrow hole? But if it was The Hulk, someone must have helped him. Who? Vattan?

Sathi pulls out a cigarette and starts unrolling it. His face burns with shame. His hands itch to tear the soda man's head from his body and throw it to the dogs. His heart pounds away, calling for revenge. Sathi stuffs ganja into the unrolled cigarette with a fury he has never known before.

The betel-nut man turns to the soda man.

—Uncle, can't be The Hulk. He couldn't have got through that hole.

The soda man's face drops. Sanmugan pipes up.

—Vattan's not here either.

—They did it together. Treacherous dogs! Sons of dogs! I gave them money whenever they asked and this is what I get for it. I'll cut their bloody stomachs open if I see them. Sons of whores!

It is time for the matinee show. The soda man knows that work must go on. He starts to clear up the mess. Sanmugan helps him. They gather the wreckage from inside and throw it out. They empty out the water tank, scrub it hard and fill it with fresh water. Next, the bottles. The soda man soaps and rinses them. But it doesn't help.

A dead, dry voice

He must invest again in the shop. He knows it, and burns with frustration.

Sathi sits there, watching everything. The soda man has not called him to help. He hasn't offered either. He must do something about his burning stomach. Maybe drink a cup of tea. Eat. Or just sleep. Maybe eat and then sleep. But he does not even have the energy to walk to the tea shop.

He gets up and goes to the water tank. He drinks until his stomach feels full. Now he can sleep. At night, he'll go to the market area to eat. He has ten rupees—poster money.

Sathi walks into the queue passage. He spreads a large poster on the floor, picks up a cloth bundle for a pillow and settles down. He lights a bidi and watches the smoke curl up to the ceiling. The passage is dark, except for rays of light filtering through. More dusk than dark. He likes the feel of twilight.

No Natesan. No Hulk. Why stay here, then? What's left for him? He looks around. Alone in all this space. With himself, all alone. Empty. He looks at the door at the far end, leading out of the passage. It seems to be saying something to him.

—Sathi, my child . . .

His father. Is he out there? On the other side of the door?

—Sathi, Sathi, don't let go . . . Sathi, it hurts, Sathi . . .

Natesan holding on to him, hugging him. Natesan pulling him by the hair. Natesan lying on the ground, curved into a ball, his body twisted with pain. White-faced, ribs crushed. No more words from his mouth after that. Just bleating sounds, a lamb whose throat is being cut.

Sathi remembers the hospital. Waiting for Natesan to wake up. Natesan's grandmother. She held him and wept. The next morning, they were gone. Grandmother and Natesan—no one knows what happened. Maybe the soda man arranged something.

Maybe even worse.

Sathi holds Natesan's cry of pain in his head like a scar. It erupts from time to time, screaming to be heard.

Sathi sits up. He walks down the passage to the outside door and pushes it open firmly. There is a crowd outside. He shuts the door behind him and looks around.

—Sathi, give me a hand. It is the cot-shop woman. She has a huge basket on her head. Sathi helps her put the basket down. The old woman begins to arrange her wares.

—Sathi! What happened to your face?

No, he can't take it. Not any more. His head down, eyes down, he cries. He doesn't look up at all. The tears come in huge waves, his chest bursts with their weight. The old woman is alarmed.

—Dai, Sathi, dai!

She puts her hand on his head and strokes him gently. He looks up, but cannot speak. He sits down, leans against the broken leg of the cot and buries his face in his hands. The old woman looks on, but soon returns to her wares.

He looks up after what seems a very long time.

Tea. He'll drink a cup and then sneak away. He gets up, dusting the mud from his hands.

—Sathi . . . dai! Sathivelu!

The soda man's voice, calling out to him.

Sathi is already near the gate. Just a few yards and he'll be out. He must walk on. Take no notice of that voice.

—Come here, Sathi. Come on!

The voice stops him for a moment.

He is not sure if he should turn and look. The voice grows louder, it comes at him sharply, aiming for his heart.

A dead, dry voice. It echoes from Meenal Theatre to Pasavur. And from other places. Places that swirl in his head. Maybe from a single place, even.

The queue passages, the doors, Natesan, The Hulk . . . the soda man, the film-reel man, ganja, darkness, piss-soaked earth, Karuvachi . . .

No escaping them. They pursue him in tight, dirty spaces.

Something soft flies at him and hits him. A dirty cloth bundle, full of lice. The lice burst out, crawling all over his face, his chest. He tries to scratch them out of his eyes, his cheeks. He wants to peel off his face.

—Dai, Sathi!

It is the soda man.

Sathi hesitates, then turns and looks back at the shop.